LISA LANTREE

Not That Professional

Contents

Chapter 1

C harlene McCay is an ambitious young celebrity news reporter at CandidExposé News. Her demeanor is relaxed, warm, and approachable, and she has a smile and confidence that attracts the crowd's attention without even trying.

Charlene does not date just anybody. She's suffered enough heartbreak that she's wary of becoming involved, especially in ways that could lead to something deeper. Instead, she chooses to throw herself into her work — writing articles, interviewing people, and investigating other people's love lives while meticulously keeping her own out of sight. It's the perfect refuge: secure, controlled, and exactly where a cautious girl like her feels most at ease. As a reporter, her creativity extends beyond her writing to the way she uncovers stories. Her genuine curiosity, sharp listening skills, and instinct for asking the right questions at just the right moment foster trust, inviting people to open up. She has a talent for drawing out even the most guarded secrets with ease.

Charlene's auburn curls tumble freely in a cascading wave, which she tames with a simple scrunchie, striking the perfect balance between elegance and practicality. Her large ocean-blue eyes seem to catch every detail, no matter how subtle. A scatter of faint freckles brushes across her nose and cheeks, lending her a natural warmth that makes her seem both youthful and grounded. Her wardrobe reflects her meticulous nature, favoring a palette of gray, black, and deep blue, tones that exude confidence and understated power. Altogether, her features blend into an effortless beauty, not demanding attention, but easily receiving it. While these features enhance her presence, her most remarkable trait is her vivid imagination—a boundless source of creativity that transforms ordinary moments into extraordinary ones.

Charlene's day starts with her trusty, vintage alarm clock—a chunky, brass thing with two bells perched on her nightstand, right next to a stack of half-read books, a tangle of charging cables, and an ever-present glass of water. As the alarm rings with an obnoxious clatter, it sounds like the start of a chaotic symphony, echoing through the room. Without fail, she groggily slaps at it, attempting to turn it off, until it crashes to the floor with a loud jangle. She finally reaches down and turns it off. Noticing the time, she stumbles out of bed and heads to the bathroom, where a quick splash of cold water and a vigorous brushing of teeth serve as her wake-up ritual, the cool water jolting her into action. After a quick shower, she hastily dresses in her work clothes, her best figure-complementing navy-blue suit jacket, a pleated knee-length skirt, and a white shirt. After gracing her face with a light layer of cosmetics, she pinches her cheeks to give them a rosy appeal—a habit she picked up from her mom's morning ritual. She catches a glimpse of the clock on the wall, realizing she is running late, she scurries down the stairs, grabs a coffee, dashes out like a caffeine-fueled whirlwind, starts her car, and drives off in her small, light blue SUV.

CandidExposé News is a news reporting company located in the heart of New York, covering celebrity news across America and worldwide. The company name is ironic and fitting, as it suggests interviews that start candidly and professionally, only to uncover shocking revelations that captivate and sometimes astonish the audience, balancing wholesome storytelling with hard-hitting exposés.

Charlene arrives at the CandidExposé parking lot in record time. She checks her wristwatch and realizes that, with all the rushing, she is still running late for work. She locates a parking spot, quickly hops out, and locks her car door. Ahead of her, she sees that the pathway to the front door of the office building is clear. A bit of a natural daydreamer, she envisions herself strolling toward the front entrance, exuding an air of calm and poise.... with each step, her heels tap softly against the pavement, the rhythm of her walk cool and professional. She navigates the lot with effortless elegance. She scans the ground ahead. A stray soda can rolls towards her, propelled by the breeze, but she sidesteps it with a deft pirouette. Then, a sudden flurry of wind sends a tumbleweed of leaves skittering across her path. She glances at it, and with a light-hearted smile, she glides around the small whirlwind as if it were an obstacle in a waltz. Her skirt flows around her in a fluid motion, almost like a dancer's costume in mid-performance. After that, a group of excited children on their way to the ice cream truck parked nearby burst into a happy commotion. And she gracefully adjusts her course, moving like a swan in a lake, giving the children a warm, knowing smile as they chatter and giggle. As she nears the front entrance of the office building, a wayward pigeon struts across her path, pecking at a crumb. She pauses, watching it for a moment before gently stepping aside. The bird flies off, and she continues her journey with the same serene grace. Reaching the building's entrance, she opens the door with a soft push, her movements as smooth as silk. She pauses just inside, turning to glance back at the parking lot with a sense of quiet triumph. Despite the little surprises the day had tossed her way, she had navigated them all with elegance and poise, like a dancer moving flawlessly through a well-rehearsed routine.

"Alright," Charlene thinks aloud, snapping out of her daydream. She is convinced she will arrive at the door unencumbered. She straightens her jacket, takes a deep breath, and makes her move. But, suddenly, just as with every morning, people seemingly come from out of nowhere; pedestrians, construction workers, and kids with balloons crossing her path. "Oops! Excuse me. On your left," she calls out, seemingly bumping into everyone on the way to the door. She navigates the bustling walkway, weaving in and out of the crowd, brushing shoulders with pedestrians, and accidentally stepping on a few toes along the way. "Hey, hey!" and "Watch it!" people cry out. Finally, she arrives, steps over the threshold, and enters the building, breathing deeply. Now, inches from the time clock, she punches her time card with just a few seconds to spare. But she is not completely unscathed - she looks down and realizes she's got a glob of strawberry ice cream trailing across the front of her jacket. She scoffs and makes an impromptu trip to the ladies' room for a cleanup. After a few minutes, she exits the restroom quickly, stumbling a little. She sighs and gathers herself together before continuing to her cubicle.

In the next cubicle, decorated with twinkling fairy lights and celebrity posters, sits her friend and co-worker, Val Kirkley. She's dressed in a shimmery fuchsia business suit, accessorized with a massive diamond-inlaid brooch, a matching necklace,

4

earrings, and even a tiara that could make a royal family envious. Her multicolored hair, reminiscent of a rainbow-dipped apple, adds an extra splash of flair as she chats on the phone, spinning lazily in her chair.

Besides being an interesting and witty, fashion-forward party goer, Val is also a talented reporter with a remarkable gift for uncovering intriguing story ideas. She crafts her articles with a distinctive blend of sophistication and flair, incorporating her fashion sense into every article, making her storytelling both impressive and admired across the office.

Val's children are grown and have flown the nest, leaving her with years of wisdom she's always eager to share with Charlene. She's never shy about offering a helping hand or imparting her expertise, whether Charlene asks for it or not.

Chapter 2

C harlene enters the office and swiftly moves through the rows of cubicles. As she passes Val's cubicle, she sees Val leaning back, twisting in her chair, and talking on the phone. It would have been fine to pass Val's cubicle and visit later when Val was less busy. However, her attention was drawn to Val's choice of attire.

Charlene halts, unable to pass up the opportunity to respond to the sight. She takes a quick visual double-take, then decides to focus on just one of the many things she could mention. "Uh, what's with the rainbow hair?" she asks, gesturing to Val's voluminous, sculpted mane.

Quickly covering the phone, Val responds, in a smooth, even tone, "I just couldn't decide on a color, so I chose them all."

"Hm," Charlene says, giving the sight a moment of thought. "It looks kind of nice." Shooting a quick thumbs-up, she turns slowly and walks to her cubicle.

Val ends her call quickly and, without delay, heads to Charlene's cubicle, entering shortly behind Charlene.

For a moment, there was silence. But, as always, it doesn't take long for Val to start poking at Charlene about her love life, insisting she needs to find someone special.

Val clears her throat, clearly gearing up to speak -

"Ah, no," Charlene interrupts, pointing a firm, no-nonsense finger at her.

"What? I haven't said a word."

"Val, I see that sparkle in your eye. I already know what you are going to say, Val. I've heard it a thousand times before. Haven't I heard it a thousand times, Val? I've heard it a thousand times before. And so, no, I don't have a boyfriend. If one should happen to come along, falling from the sky or propelling from some great height, maybe it will be an exciting thing to talk about. Maybe we could even throw a party. Celebrate. Dance all night. Until then, no. Let's talk about a new topic. How about that bundle of reader mail we got just last week – we have lots of big fans, huh?"

Val pauses, sits quietly, gazing occasionally at Charlene, but says nothing. She figures that Charlene may need a moment of silence as she begins her workday. Val sighs, "Alright," resolving to give Charlene a few moments of silence. Then Val sits quietly, casually looking away to give the impression that she is not focusing on Charlene. Slowly, she begins bringing her gaze back to Charlene. She takes in Charlene's typical work outfit: a neatly pressed shirt and a ponytail. She can't resist offering a full fashion critique, playfully remarking, "Dear, you're looking... neutral, as usual."

But Charlene doesn't feel ready for the conversation. She is too busy, too uninterested. She flashes Val a quick smile and continues working, organizing her tasks for the day while thinking up a quick comical escape from the cubicle.

Val is keeping her eyes fixed on Charlene.

Preparing herself for the impending avalanche of critiques and inquiries, Charlene sighs and quips, "Alright, spill the beans. Where is this conversation going, as if I don't already know?"

Seeing an opening, Val brings up Charlene's need for romance. "I'm just curious. When are you going to find a date? You haven't been dating in a long while."

"An aunt?" Charlene laughs. "Val, we're not sisters."

"Where are you getting this from, dear? Yes, we are," Val insisted with heartfelt conviction. "Aren't we all sisters at heart?" she says, her words dipped in the sweet syrup of empathy.

Finding no compelling reason for her best friend to cease her playful encouragement, Charlene chuckles, shrugs, and nods in agreement.

"So, come on," Val continues. "What do you think?
I know somebody."

"Oh, no, no, no, my dear, Val. Do you recall the last blind date you set me up with? Filbert? He hummed every time he took a sip of his drink."

"Well, that can be kind of cute."

"Cute? Mmm," Charlene hums, "not really."

"Oh."

"And the guy before that, Robrick? That's a new name for me. Yeah, he attempted to feed me his meal, like a little baby bird, from his mouth."

Just then, Charlene's cameraman, Clay, peeks in from around the corner and chuckles, "From his mouth? Sweet! I've got to try that."

Charlene shudders, and Val laughs.

"That's enough, Clay," Charlene scoffs with a bit of rye humor. "Ladies are talking," she says blocking his view with paperwork. Charlene sees Clay as a kind of little brother, and she tries to protect his delicate, impressionable ears.

"Ok, ok," Clay says, taking the hint. He walks away quipping,

"I don't know how else I'm going to get all of these great dating tips unless I'm listening to you, ladies."

Charlene and Val chuckle.

Clay, Charlene's young college-age cameraman, is a skilled and dedicated individual with a keen eye for capturing compelling videos and always seeking the perfect shot. With his technical expertise and creative flair, he consistently delivers high-quality footage. He is the secret weapon of Charlene's team, and he's not shy about it, strutting around with his camera ready for action, like a boss, knowing he's the Michelangelo of videography.

Clay has wavy ash-brown hair and a youthful face. His wardrobe consists of practical pieces that facilitate easy movement while he captures footage - a plain white t-shirt adorned with a duck print design, complemented by dark denim jeans. His comfortable clothing choices prioritize functionality over fashion.

Val persists in her scrutiny of Charlene. "You're positively radiating professionalism," she remarks, miming a spectacular yawn for added flair. "Don't you have some fun clothes somewhere?"

"What? And, wear them to work?"

"(Scoff) Ye-es."

"I am not dressed too professionally. My blouse has ruffles," Charlene says, pointing at the thin ruffle trim on the wrists and collar of her blouse.

"No, you're dressed professional lite. I bet If I passed you a napkin, I'd get it back neatly pressed and folded."

Charlene smirks, holding back a chuckle.

"It's just that I haven't seen you dating in a long time. I think you should loosen up a bit, maybe come to work in jeans once in a while." Val continues. "Huh? So, what are you waiting for? Come on. Let me take you to my favorite boutique."

"You know, Val, you are starting to sound like my mom," Charlene sighs.

"Not your mom, dear," Val corrects, "more like your love advisor."

"Again, my dear friend, no-o. And, what's wrong with what I have on? Professionally, it's perfect for work; it's comfortable, breathable, functional..."

Val rolls her eyes. "Yeah, that's what's wrong with it," she replies. "You need something, a feel-good outfit. I know a pretty girl is under there somewhere. You should change your look, Charlie."

"That's it. You know, only my mom calls me Charlie. You've been hanging out with my mom - no, she's in Tennessee. Are you channeling my mom? You are channeling my mom." Charlene stood quietly in front of the diamond-angled mirror by her desk, gazing at her fashion-subdued image, thinking maybe this time, Val is right. She may need a change of some kind. "Maybe," she says quietly, gazing at her reflection.

"Doggone right! Now, go ahead. Treat yourself to some couture," Val suggests, striking a pose while proudly showcasing her elegant brooch, trying to flash a little of its sparkle into Charlene's eyes for effect.

"Val. I mean, who's got the budget for couture?" Charlene asks as she plops resignedly into her office chair. She raises an eyebrow and, suddenly throwing Val a quizzical gaze, asks, "Do you?"

"Of course not, dear. I know people. And when you know people, you can borrow things," Val responds with an air of worldly sophistication and a smile. "It's practical, resourceful, and cost-effective," she says, throwing a hand up for emphasis. "We have the most enjoyable time closet diving." Val pauses and once again eyes Charlene's clothing. "Hm, we'll have to make it a group activity sometime."

Chapter 3

J ust then, Charlene's boss, Horace Rudger, calls Charlene to his office. Still seated, Charlene peers out over the cubicle wall. She calls out, "What's up?" She can tell from his tone that whatever the issue is, it must be serious.

Horace gives her a forceful gesture to come into his office, then disappears distractedly into it.

"Oh boy, what did you do?" chided Val cooly.

"What did I do? What did you do?" Charlene retorts, flipping her hair before strutting over to Horace's office. Once she gets there, she straightens up for a more professional appearance.

Charlene slips into the room without a sound, keeping her eyes on Horace and closing the door behind her. Her mind is blank, unsure of what is happening. Horace's office has long since lost its simplicity and is now busy with the history of CandidExposé News. A massive collage adorns the wall next to the door, showcasing the triumphant tales of his top writers. The collage serves as a visual testament to their success and dedication. The sill of the large single window in the room is lined with numerous awards, further highlighting his appreciation for excellence.

Horace, a powerfully built individual with a commanding presence, paces behind his desk like a caged tiger or a pissed bear. His imposing stature is not diminished by his diagonally striped tie, or grey jacket and pants. His eyes are fixed on the pile of assignments on his desk. His arms are tightly crossed over his chest, his fingers tapping rhythmically.

The sunlight pouring in through the window behind him shines on his slightly silvery, slightly frayed hair, making him look like an ancient wizard in a modern-day office suit. His furrowed brow and the slight frown on his face reveal his growing frustration. The tension in his body is palpable as if he is ready to spring into action at any moment.

Completely out of curiosity after sensing the tension, a few other reporters gather outside Horace's office and intently listen in through the door.

Charlene wonders about the issue, but before she can ask again, Horace blurts out, "I have a story for you." He quickly grabs a file from his desk. "It's an important one. So, you cannot blow this."

"Horace," Charlene scoffs, "I don't blow any stories. You know that. When was the last time I blew any stories? I don't blow any stories."

Horace begins rattling off stories: "The countess's blue pearl earrings, a surprise birthday gift that came up in your interview and was no longer a surprise.

And the time you brought a wedding gift to celebrity June Price's baby shower when nobody knew the sex of the baby. You brought pink booties."

"Okay, fine. Two, out of hundreds of stories! Hundreds of stories!"

"And, then there was the time-"

"Ok, ok," Charlene relents, rolling her eyes. Hoping not to have her quirky reruns played back, she asks, "Alright then, what's this all about?"

"I need you to write a story on Allen Howser," Horace says, passing her a manila folder with an 8 x 10 professional headshot of Allen, paperclipped to the front. "The story is, heart-throb Allen Howser is seeing millionairess Gina Tarvec, and he is now off the market. He's been very elusive."

"In his case, evasive is a better word," Charlene mutters.

"Elusive, evasive, both," Horace responds, revealing his keen sense of hearing.

"We need you to find out for sure if there is anything there."

"Of course," Charlene replies.

"Yeah, I know you're not a fan, and that's what makes you the perfect reporter for this story. I considered people. But that quality of yours might help you to get close enough to him to ask him a few questions. I know for sure you won't be drooling on his shoes like some of our other reporters. So, you've got to give us a good story." Horace looks at Charlene seriously. "You know you haven't given us a home run story in a while, and we need you on this one."

Disputing again, Charlene says, "I tend to disagree. What about the story from two weeks ago, actress Le-, Leilani Hale winning that award after her big movie debut?"

"And you couldn't seem to pronounce her first name right. You kept calling her Leeloo. Leeloo. Who is Leeloo?" Horace folds his arms across his chest again. "And now that the cameras are off, you can pronounce her name right?"

"I've been practicing."

Horace relents, "Okay, fine. I'll give you that one. But you can't stay in la-la land, living out your glory days. We've got stories to tell. And it's your job to keep the stories coming in. Come on. We're seriously getting heat in the outfield from the director. And that means you've got to knock it out of the park."

Horace is a big baseball fan, and anytime he uses baseball analogies, Charlene knows he is either serious or impatient. Maybe it's a combination of both today.

"Just find out what's going on," Horace says sternly. "Find out how serious they are. Are there any wedding plans? Bring back a winning story. Got it?"

"Got it," Charlene responds.

"Swing away."

Charlene's coworkers possess a sixth sense for her imminent return to the door, and like startled squirrels, they dart away or suddenly transform into the busiest bees in the office hive!

As Charlene leaves Horace's office, she notices several colleagues moving away from the door, some pretending to file papers or sharpen pencils, acting nonchalantly as they coolly glance at her. A few of them give her a knowing nod - that special impressed look that screams, "You've just hit the jackpot of assignments!"

Charlene responds with a reassuring grin, wisely brushing off their bewildered expressions and hushed chatter. She straightens her posture before striding confidently toward her cubicle.

Charlene is tasked with writing a story about Allen Howser, a popular action star and notorious bachelor who is wildly evasive of media attention. Despite the rumors of a new love interest, Allen is difficult to reach for interviews. The press has been unable to get close to him, adding to the challenge of Charlene's assignment.

Dryly, Charlene mutters, "Fantastic," as she ponders how to interview the most elusive actor ever to grace the public eye.

Val gives Charlene a long look as she returns to her desk, "I could hear the yelling from here," she says through the cubicle wall. Val puts the finishing touches on her assignment, holding her pen like an artist's paintbrush.

"Really?" asks Charlene, with a grin and a look of disbelief.

"Well, I didn't hear the words, but whatever it was about, at least I didn't hear any baseball counting strikes, again. And that's good."

Charlene let out a sigh that could rival a deflating balloon and leaned back in her chair.

"He didn't, did he?"

"Of course, he did, Val. In all our years of knowing him, when has he ever not?"

"Well, there was that one time... you know? The coffee spill."

"Yeah, but he wasn't in the office at the time."

"Oh, yeah," Val recalls. Just then, her face lights up with excitement and curiosity. She turns her gaze towards Charlene. "Well, don't keep me in suspense! Who are you interviewing?"

"Allen Howser."

"Oh, you are a lucky, lucky girl," Val responds with a smile. Val slips into a daydream, quietly fanning herself.

"Uh, Val, I think you're drooling," says Charlene with a smirk.

"Oh," Val says, snapping out of her trance. "You do know that an interview with him is a career-maker, don't you? Because nobody can get a hold of him. He's too quick. He's in and out so quickly! He's like that bartender on Sunset with the quick hands, you know the one."

"Samuel."

"Yeah. I like watching him work. Wonder if he's free."

"Val, focus."

"Anyway, I hope Allen isn't that fast in bed," Val says to Charlene's surprise.

Surprised, Charlene looks at Val and smiles, then returns to business: "Well, I need to find out if he is seeing millionairess Gina Tarvec."

"Oh, the nasal talker."

"She's not a nasal talker," Charlene corrects, attempting to keep the conversation polite.

Val snickers a little, with a snort.

"Well, maybe a little bit. She has her own unique way of speaking."

"Yeah-h," Val says slowly. "Well, I hear she's from old money. Her family owns Tarvec Properties. They are big in the world of Real Estate and Finance." Val pauses. "So, that's the story, to find out if Allen and Gina are a couple?"

"That's the story," Charlene says. Charlene points to a page in the manila folder, "According to this, they've been seen a few places together." She flips a page and reads through the information like a doctor analyzing a perplexing medical case.

"Handsome bachelor, Allen Howser. Wow," Val says with dreamy wide eyes and a big grin.

"Right," Charlene says. "You know, Horace says he considered people for this interview."

"He says he's considered people?" asks Val. "He's always considering people. What? That's his job. What's new? I've considered people for jobs. Who hasn't?" Val says, rolling her eyes. Then she notices Charlene's pensive look, "Aren't you excited? You're going to meet handsome bachelor, actor, and action star, Allen Howser. You don't seem excited. What-? What did I say? Did I break something? Shake your head, let me check."

"Oh, cut it out," Charlene chuckles. She puts the paperwork onto her desktop and says, "I'm not a fan."

"What do you mean you're not a fan?"

"I mean, I am not a fan. I don't think much of his acting skills. His delivery is poor, and I think he takes too many risks because he insists on performing his own stunts."

"Charlene, Charlene, Charlene," Val sighs. "Ok, the way you feel about this interviewee is not new. It's a job. We know how to handle it, right? Be professional. You know, be cool. So, what are you going to do?"

They sit silently looking at each other for a moment.

"Charlie?" asks Val, tapping her freshly manicured nails on the desktop.

"I am going to make this story work."

"What's that?' Val says enthusiastically.

"I just said it. I am going to make this story work!"

"That a girl!"

"I'm going to get out there, and I'm going to own this story."

"Good for you. Now that you have this story to work on, how about we celebrate," Val says. "Beverages at CroonEoke's tonight. My treat."

"Beverages, Val?" asks Charlene, a little surprised. "Where are we now, at La Oy-Stir Club Du Jour?"

"Well, yeah, you know. Shots."

"Thank you, Val, but not tonight. I'm going to get started on this story."

"Great!" Val exclaims excitedly, gearing up to inject Charlene's already buzzing enthusiasm with an extra dose of inspirational oomph. "Go on and write that story. You've got this."

Chapter 4

That evening, Charlene and her cameraman, Clay, set out to find the elusive, almost reclusive Allen.

Allen is just arriving in town to finish a shoot for his upcoming movie called Superspy Returns: Home by Midnight. His plane has just landed, and he is attempting to get to his limo to leave the airport. He is surrounded by reporters who want to interview him about his connection with Gina Tarvec.

Charlene and Clay know that Allen doesn't like to be interviewed, so they decide to stay back and observe.

Allen is practically a walking, talking heartthrob on-screen. With his chiseled jawline, piercing blue eyes, and perfectly styled shiny, dark brown hair, he effortlessly captures the spotlight every time he graces the screen. His robust physique and chiseled muscles reveal his unwavering dedication to action stunts.. He shines in heroic roles, which are also his all-time favorite parts to tackle. Enthusiastic fans eagerly gather around him wherever he goes. Whether performing daring stunts, pulling off spontaneous antics, or delivering powerful performances, Allen's talent and charisma shine through. His unpredictable, larger-than-life personality only fuels his popularity, as fans love to see what he'll do next—both on and off the screen.

Although he has a few bodyguards for support, Allen is not

one for bodyguards; instead, he relies on his quick wit and a trusty hoodie. A hoodie is his go-to "stealth mode" in the wild jungle of crowds – it's like his personal invisibility cloak, and it's surprisingly effective on top of a t-shirt and jeans. He wears a no-slip grip for smooth getaways, a black leather belt cinches his waist, and a silver wristwatch, which hasn't kept time since the dawn of time, adorns his wrist.

Allen values his privacy, but as a celebrity, he is constantly hounded by reporters who want to know every detail of his life. To avoid them, he is quick to perform wild stunts with the objects around him, which he knows not only help him escape but also excite onlookers. Now, he appears cornered, surrounded by a group of reporters.

As Charlene and Clay watch, they notice that Allen avoids eye contact with the reporters. Charlene wants to approach him and ask for an interview; however, she knows he will decline. But, in her mind, she imagines, he wouldn't decline an interview; on the contrary, he would seek an interview... with her... In the realm of her imagination, Allen Howser, the dazzling actor known for his blockbuster roles and charming smile, is caught in a whirlwind of flashing cameras and excited reporters clamoring for his attention outside the studio. It is a typical chaotic scene, with everyone shouting questions and jostling to grab a quote from the star. But, amidst the frenzy, Allen's eyes scan the crowd like a hawk searching for its prey. His expression is a mix of amusement and determination. It isn't just any interview he is after; there is one reporter he has in mind—Charlene. As reporters hurl questions at him about his latest film and his rumored love life, Allen remains unfazed. He navigates through the throngs of journalists with the grace of a dance partner, all the while keeping his gaze fixed on one person: Charlene, who is subtly trying to blend into the background of the chaos. "Ms. Charlene! Where's Ms. Charlene?" Allen calls out, his voice cutting through the cacophony. Charlene, who has been cleverly trying to avoid the spotlight, suddenly finds herself the center of attention. She is about to duck behind a particularly tall cameraman when she hears Allen's voice. With a mixture of surprise and mild panic, Charlene raises her hand. "Here!" she calls, though she is trying to stay as inconspicuous as possible. Allen's face lights up like a kid in a candy store. He points directly at her. "There she is!" he declares triumphantly, like he's just discovered buried treasure. The crowd falls silent, bewildered. Reporters stare, mouths agape, as Allen makes a beeline for Charlene, leaving the others in stunned confusion. He moves with the grace and poise of a superhero, almost bouncing, and he approaches her with a wide grin. He ignores the dismayed murmurs from his entourage. "Charlene, I've been looking for you," Allen says as if they were old friends meeting after a long time apart. "I only want to do this interview with you."

Charlene blinks, momentarily flustered. "Oh, um, okay! I'm happy to—"

Before she can finish, Allen grabs her arm and pulls her gently towards a quieter corner away from the press. As they walk, reporters try to follow, but Allen's personal security team forms an effective barrier.

Once they are out of earshot, Charlene can't help but laugh. "So, Mr. Howser, what's this all about?"

Allen shrugs, his smile never fading. "I hear that you are the best at turning a simple interview into an experience. And honestly, I just want to see if it is true."

Charlene chuckles, "Well, I'm flattered. Let's see if we can make this interview as memorable as you hoped!"

And with that, the chaos of the crowd fades into the background as Charlene and Allen sit down for what would undoubtedly become one of the most talked-about interviews of the year—proving once again that sometimes, the best stories are the ones that start with a little bit of unexpected drama and a lot of good humor.

Charlene is immediately awakened from her daydream by a quick but firm nudge from Clay, "Get that," Clay says excitedly, pointing toward Allen, "I think he is going to give an interview this time."

"I'm not so sure."

"I'd bet my hat."

Standing nearby, they can see Allen clearly through the crowd. He speaks loudly and firmly. "I am not interested in an interview, right now," he says. "Contact my agent." But this only seems to spur them on. Suddenly, Allen bids them all a good day, and with some quick thinking and the grace of one of his on-screen personas, he grabs a nearby trash can and uses it to vault over their heads. He then runs toward a nearby construction site and climbs a crane, followed closely by astonished reporters. Equally astonished, Charlene and Clay join in the chase.

"I owe you a hat," Clay says.

"Keep it. You can eat it."

In a fleeting moment, Charlene and Allen's eyes meet just briefly before he disappears behind the crane. All the reporters were left behind, unable to keep up with him. Allen felt a sense of relief as he escaped their prying eyes once again.

"He just acted out the mad escape scene from his movie, The Swashbuckler Reborn! Didn't he? Didn't he? Wow! That was cool," Clay says in amazement. Charlene rolls her eyes, figuring this won't be an easy gig.

Chapter 5

The park is adorned with vibrant, flowering pink, yellow, and purple shrubs, creating a picturesque scene. The morning sun's golden rays filter through the lush green leaves of the trees, casting a warm glow on the surroundings. The gentle breezes rustle through the branches, carrying the sweet fragrance of blooming flowers. Sounds of chirping birds fill the air, adding a melodic touch to the serene atmosphere. Families and friends are gathered on the well-manicured lawns, enjoying picnics and laughter. The scene is a harmonious blend of nature's wonders and human joy, creating a wonderful sight in the park.

Charlene and Clay are sitting in a grey work van, which they use to stake out their stories. It has a spacious interior, two front seats, and a large cargo area in the back. The van has tinted windows for privacy and a built-in GPS for navigation. Inside are multiple compartments and storage areas to keep their equipment organized, which also happen to be the perfect fit for their snacks and coffee. Overall, the work van provides Charlene and Clay with a comfortable and practical space to conduct their stakeouts and pursue their stories.

With a mouthful of doughnuts, Clay quips, "You know what they say, doughnuts are the ultimate brain food!" Clay smiles with his cheeks full of a sweet, delicious morsel. "Although they could use a dash of vitamins to make it official!"

Clay offers Charlene a doughnut, but Charlene is completely distracted. Using a pair of binoculars, Charlene spots Allen across the park, disguised in a headband and hoodie, going for a jog. She knows it is him, but she also knows she can't confront him directly. Not yet. She needs a plan.

The next morning, with Clay waiting behind, she climbs out of the work van and follows Allen, keeping a safe distance, watching him as he runs. She figures if she can casually chat with Allen in such a serene outdoor setting, she can get more information for her story.

Adhering to a professional appearance, Charlene wears a jogging outfit of understated greys, carefully chosen for the occasion of meeting Allen on his morning jog. She slips on a headband to hold her hair in place. Now, she feels ready for action.

The moment has arrived. Allen casually jogs through the park, maintaining a steady pace as he navigates the winding paths and lush greenery. His strides are relaxed yet purposeful, effortlessly gliding across the pavement. With each step, his feet lightly touch the ground, creating a rhythmic pattern that matches the beat of his favorite playlist playing through his earphones. The morning sunlight filters through the trees, casting a warm glow on his face as he breathes in the fresh air. Allen's posture is relaxed, his shoulders loose, and his arms swinging naturally at his sides. He occasionally gives long nods or waves at familiar faces he encounters along his journey and exchanges brief greetings with a friendly smile.

Charlene imagines their meeting.... She times her approach perfectly, walking towards him with confidence and ease. As

Allen nears, she offers a warm, genuine smile and greets him with a friendly "Hello" that feels casual yet deliberate. Without breaking his stride, Allen slows down, intrigued by her relaxed demeanor. Charlene strikes the perfect balance between light conversation and curiosity, quickly finding common ground in their shared love for the outdoors. The encounter feels effortless, and their connection is immediate, as if their paths were meant to cross in that moment - a perfect first encounter.

As he comes near her vicinity, Charlene snaps out of her daydream. Eager to catch his attention, she strategically positions herself along his jogging route and carefully times her movements to coincide with his approach. However, despite her efforts, Charlene's timing is slightly off, and she narrowly misses Allen as he passes. Did he anticipate her? In unexpected energy and determination, she pivots on her heel and takes off in hot pursuit, sprinting after him for several hundred yards.

Despite her valiant effort, he somehow employs some uncanny escape artistry, slipping through her grasp and leaving her breathless and frustrated in his wake. It seems to her that he knows what she is up to.

Upon returning to the van, Clay inquires whether she managed to catch up with Allen. She turns to Clay, her face a blend of dry humor and drenched disappointment, all too vividly conveying the answer – a resounding "no." Frustrated, and between breaths, she gasps, chokes out a cough, and asks, "What is it? Does he practice running with deer?"

Clay snickers.

Chapter 6

As the sun peeks over the horizon, Charlene and Clay find themselves in full stakeout mode, positioned just outside Allen's residence. Then, out of the blue, a squad of Clay's youthful pals roll up to the van, having spotted it from a mile away. Dressed in signature jeans, casual tees, and well-worn sneakers, they pound on the van's window, unleashing a playful barrage of banter on Clay. "Hey there, Clay! Who's your target tonight?" they taunt, and one of his friends cheekily adds, "Dude, snap a pic of me. I want to put it on social media!" amid chuckles and camaraderie.

Clay plays the introducer, gesturing toward his friends and saying, "Charlene, meet the rowdy crew: Duffy, Max, and Lenny." Charlene's stunning presence leaves them all visibly impressed, and their eyes ping-pong back and forth between her and each other like spectators at a tennis match, each of them vying for the ideal moment to start a playful conversation with her, while silently debating who should take the first shot.

Clay explains to Charlene, "Despite their appearance, these college-age individuals have their unique aspirations. Each one of them is driven by their own set of goals and dreams. They are motivated to achieve success in their respective fields and make a difference in the world." Clay gestures with his hand, as though explaining the importance of flavor in a succulent dish. "They are determined to work hard and overcome any obstacles that come their way. Their aspirations range from pursuing a career helping others to making a mark in the world of technology and innovation to becoming an influential figure in the arts and creativity. These individuals have a clear vision of what they want to accomplish and are dedicated to turning their aspirations into reality."

"Oh, they're musicians in a band. Got it," Charlene says with a smile and a nod. "That's cool."

Immediately, Duffy is drawn to Charlene. He stands at the crossroads of rugged charm and untamed spirit. His red hair radiates like a blazing sunset, hinting at a personality equally vibrant and unyielding. His attire speaks of a carefree attitude, favoring well-worn jeans and a threadbare t-shirt that has seen it's fair share of adventures. His eyes sparkle with mischief as if he's perpetually prepared to cannonball into a pool of shenanigans.

Duffy is drawn to Charlene's polite smile, but she shifts her focus again, peering across the street into Allen's window. "Oh, so that's who you're checking out, that Allen dude," he says with a nod. "You know, I'd be a better choice than that guy. I do parkour," he proudly says to Charlene. He flexes his muscles as he goes over to block her view of Allen's place.

"You jump rope and play basketball, Duffy," Clay corrects with a smirk.

Duffy lets out a barely audible harrumph, brushing off Clay's interruption entirely. "Tut, tut, my good friend. I perform on weekends at the mall."

"Weekends at the mall? Oh, you mean skateboarding."

"Hey, don't mess up my action," Duffy says, and he continues flirting with Charlene. "Well, what do you say? Would you like to go out with me?" he asks, seizing the moment.

Charlene smiles and promptly responds, "No, thanks. Shouldn't you be at home studying? Now, go on, I've got work to do."

"You sure?" he asks with a smile, smacking his lips.

"I am sure."

"Alright, then," Duffy says as he heads off with his friends, but not without giving Charlene another glimpse of his physique, walking past her like a bodybuilder. "Yeah, you want this," he says softly with a smile.

Charlene tries not to laugh but closes her eyes and pretends to cough.

Shortly thereafter, Charlene rambles on to Clay, telling him, "If I can expose the truth behind their relationship, it is really going to be a boost to my career!" Suddenly, she notices Clay is gazing past her out of the window as if he's just seen a dancing buffalo in a tutu.

"Wow," Clay says under his breath. He starts swiftly and skillfully preparing his camera without looking at it.

Charlene's heart begins to race as Clay motions toward Allen's place. Charlene looks and finds Allen standing with the beautiful millionairess, Gina Tarvec. Gina has a tall, slender physique. Her blond hair, touched with subtle highlights, frames her face with a tousled, carefree elegance. She wears a casual blouse and wide-leg pants. She looks like a supermodel, as if she had just stepped out of a magazine photo shoot.

Charlene can't decide whether to be impressed or to suspect that Gina might be an alien from a planet where perfection is the norm.

Chapter 7

Charlene is watching Allen and Gina from the van. As a journalist, Charlene is looking to reveal a sensational story. She quickly begins formulating a plan in her head, considering all the angles she could take to make this story captivating. Despite her excitement, she remains composed and focused on the task. This is her chance to make a name for herself, and she isn't going to let it slip away.

Gina's limousine is picking her up from Allen's place. Allen and Gina kiss each other on the cheek before she leaves. Charlene is intent on getting the story.

The next day, Charlene sits on a park bench pretending to tie her shoelaces. She casually unties them and ties them again for the fourth time, her eyes scanning the path ahead. She waits patiently, her anticipation palpable. She knows that Allen is due to pass by any moment now.

Charlene taps her foot nervously, her fingers drumming on her thigh. The sound of footsteps grows louder, and her heart skips a beat. Finally, Allen comes into view, his rhythmic strides bringing him closer. Charlene's face lights up with a smile as he nears. She stretches her legs out in an artificial yawn at the perfect moment to interrupt his progress. As she does, he nearly does an impossible mid-air barrel roll over her legs, spinning in the air like a superhero without a cape. He skillfully evades her effortlessly and continues jogging with barely a glance her way.

Clay looks on in disbelief. Charlene arrives back at the van, and Clay teases, "I think you're going to have to use tougher measures."

The next morning, Charlene is in full jogging gear, ready to meet Allen as he jogs by. She moves in front of Allen from behind a tree, blocking his pathway a few times, with an "Oops." It's beginning to look as though she's finally caught his attention, but she doesn't realize that a small bush is nearby, and she goes toppling over it, falling backward into the shrubbery.

Allen extends his hand to help Charlene stand up. She appears slightly embarrassed as she gazes up at him. Allen finds himself captivated by her unassuming appearance, with leaves and twigs in her hair. Concerned about her well-being, he says with a feigned southern accent, "You've got to be careful, miss. There're lots of wild bushes and shrubs tucked away everywhere in these parts."

"Uh, yes," Charlene chuckles, instantly recognizing his comment as a playful reference to one of his most iconic movie roles – the quirky Billy VanWhiffle in Blazing Gold Rush. It feels like a subtle, halfhearted attempt to hint at his identity. Still, she finds the gesture endearing, appreciating that he's showing concern for her.

"This is not a come-on, but you look familiar to me," Allen says. "Have we met?"

"I don't think so. I'm new to the area."

"New to the area, meaning new to this city?"

"No, I am new to this park," she laughs, dusting off her clothes. "My old haunt is across town, and honestly, I haven't been jogging for fitness in ages."

"Well, you're looking good, though," he replies.

"Whatever you're doing is agreeing with you."

"Well, thank you. Same." Charlene says politely as Allen gestures an offer to pull twigs out of her hair. "I drive everywhere. But I might jog, from time to time," she pauses and smirks, "if I'm running late."

"Exactly. It's good to get out and take in a deep breath of air. Good for the bod."

"Yeah, well, not exactly for my bum," Charlene chuckles, "but yeah."

Allen smiles, "Would you like to go for a coffee? My treat."

"Sure," she responds, pleased he asked.

Allen and Charlene make their way to the nearest coffee haven, just a stone's throw from the park. Stepping inside, they find themselves enveloped in a warm, welcoming embrace, as if the cafe itself is giving them a friendly hug. The interior exudes coziness, with rustic wooden panels adorning the walls and plush armchairs in floral prints, evoking a charming, old-world atmosphere. The cafe is abuzz with life, every table occupied by patrons engrossed in their laptops, compelling books, or lively conversations.

Chapter 8

They order their beverages with little conversation before settling at a table. Allen is quietly thrilled by the ease of their silence—it feels natural, unforced, as though words would only get in the way. Charlene, meanwhile, is pleasantly surprised by his gentlemanly manner, remembering how he held the door open for her with such simple grace.

They sip their drinks, make small talk about their interests, and marvel at the cafe's peaceful atmosphere. They both feel a comfortable connection growing. She can't help but stare as he sensually sips his coffee, and her attention drifts toward that tempting, pouty lip on his mug.

Noticing her gaze, Allen asks, "What's up?"

"Oh, uh, nothing. I was thinking you have a nice mug- I mean drinking mug."

Allen offers her a warm smile, almost bursting out laughing, and she responds with a coy smile of her own. Despite his charms, Charlene makes a conscious effort not to be overly captivated by his good looks, perfect smile, and charisma. She reminds herself about Gina, thinking, "Isn't he dating Gina?"

Figuring that Allen is not very likely to bolt from a quiet little coffee shop, Charlene seizes the golden opportunity to grill

Allen with a barrage of queries, starting with gentle, strategic inquiries to warm up the interrogation. She kicks off with the ever-so-riveting topic of weather because nothing gets the truth flowing like discussing whether it's raining cats and dogs.

He responds comfortably, "It looks like it's going to be a sunny day today. The weather report says the temperature is expected to be around 75 degrees Fahrenheit, with a slight breeze. Cooler this evening. I'd say that sounds like pleasant weather," he says, casually taking a sip of coffee.

Allen, feels more comfortable, enough to begin sharing more information about himself.

Charlene's patient and persistent style of interviewing is paying off. "And so, what do you do for a living?"

Allen responds freely, almost proudly, "I am an actor and stuntman," he says, sitting up in his chair. Wondering if she already knows it. He inquires, "Do you recognize me?"

She chokes back on coffee, nearly spitting it out, and says, "Yes. I do recognize you, actually. I just wanted to hear it from you, you know, to be sure."

"Oh." Quietly taking a sip of coffee, he then asks, "What do you think of my acting?" He is now staring deeply into her eyes as if he's expecting answers to life's greatest mysteries.

Charlene wonders why he had to ask that question. She hesitates, and then reluctantly tells him to his utter dismay, "I think you are," she hesitates, gulping down a swallow of coffee, "I think you are not a very good actor, your delivery sucks, and you take too many risks since you do your own stunts."

There was a moment of silence that seemed, to Charlene, to last an hour as he appeared to be mulling over her comment from all sides.

"Huh!" he responds quietly to himself. He is completely

caught off guard. He wasn't expecting such a direct and brutal answer, yet there it was. But there is something that he likes about her complete and total honesty. And so, throwing all his cares to the wind, he asks Charlene for a date. "Would you like to go dancing with me tonight?"

"Sure," Charlene responds after a sip of coffee. "Where?"

Charlene wonders, "Is he going to suggest CroonEoke's nightclub?"

"I know this place everybody goes to: CroonEoke's nightclub."

"Seriously?" she muses. "Uh, yes."

"Now, all I have to do is tell Val about this so she won't blow my cover," Charlene thinks, recalling that CroonEoke's is Val's favorite nightclub, and she just might show up there.

Once Charlene returns to the van, she shares the news with Clay, and he immediately erupts, unsure of Charlene's decision to go on a date with Allen. Clay feels the move is too personal and tries to get her to reconsider. He can't help but worry about the potential outcome of the date. He reminds Charlene of the dangers of getting too close to the subject. "Isn't there some unspoken rule about getting too cozy with the subject? You know," Clay says, pausing to adopt an artificially pensive look. "Like, you could become part of the story or something? You remember that big proposal story. Bob, on the second floor, got in the camera shot. The world thought he was proposing to a famous actress – he was tying his shoelaces. Yeah, they almost got married."

"What's wrong with that?"

"He's already married."

"Relax, I'm good," Charlene says. "Will you just relax? I've got this."

"And how are you going to keep it professional?"

"I don't know. But I need this story, and I am going to get close enough to get it."

Clay, now realizing the potential for a career-making great story, decides to trust Charlene's judgment.

As Charlene begins primping her hair, trying to decide on a new hairstyle, Clay can't shake the feeling of uncertainty, but he relents. "Ok, then," he says, throwing his hands up. slapping, and rubbing them together for emphasis. "Let's do this. Let's go get that story."

On the way home, Charlene calls Val and shares the news that she has a date with Allen.

Val is excited to hear the news. "You're going on a date?" she says excitedly. "At last!"

"It's just a date for a story. It's an opportunity for me to get the answers I need."

"Does he know that?"

Charlene is silent, and then, clearing her throat, she says, "I, uh-"

"It's a date." They both get quiet, "I'll be right there," Val sings, happy to share a little girl time with Charlene . She is excited for her, even if it's just a date for a story. She brings over some outfits from her closet to help Charlene look stylish.

Immediately, Val sets out several beautiful dresses, ranging from an elegant evening gown to a playful sundress. "I keep them ready for just such an occasion."

"Is that why they're labeled 'Charlene's first date dress,' 'Charlene's second date dress,' and so on?" Charlene asks. "Val, are you moonlighting as a psychic fashion consultant or just really committed to over-preparation?"

"I like being prepared. You never know," Val says as she neatly unfolds a dress. "I have a bucket list for when I win the lottery, too," she adds, smiling. "So, where are you going?"

"CroonEoke's," replies Charlene .

"Okay, then," Val resolves, "you need this one." Val passes Charlene a beautiful, radiant black pleated metallic lamé dress with a sweetheart neckline, shimmering under the lights, smiles, and puts away the other dresses. "We'll save these dresses for later."

"What's that? Did I see more labels on those dresses?" Charlene asks.

"Yes. But don't worry about it. Well? Go on, go on. Try on the dress."

Charlene tries on the dress in another room, slipping into it like a hand in a glove.

"How is it fitting?" Val calls out from the next room.

"It's a bit snug getting in, but I think I've got this," Charlene remarks, taking deep, steadying breaths. Charlene steps into view. Venturing outside of her usual professional comfort zone feels like a thrilling escape, and for a moment, she allows herself to revel in the fantasy. The dress hugs her perfectly, making her feel like a princess at a grand ball, far removed from her everyday world.

"Wow," Val says. "And, not over-dressed."

"Really?"

"Alright, maybe just a smidge," Val admits with a grin, adjusting the hem of the dress Charlene is sporting. "But it's CroonEoke's," she continues, her tone light. "Once, I entered a beauty contest there wearing a mud-splattered tank top and my favorite bell-bottom jeans. And believe it or not, I came in second place."

Charlene raises an eyebrow in disbelief. "You, the fashion icon of the decade, came in second?"

"This was well before my high-fashion awakening, my dear," replies Val quickly. "Anyway, let's live it up. Now, let's do something with your hair."

Charlene's eyes widen with a mixture of fascination and anticipation as she awaits the final reveal.

Later that evening, Allen knocks. Val peeks out of the window and sees him waiting at the door in a grey T-shirt and blue jacket.

"Wow," Val says. "Your date is here, and he has come to play," she says, changing her tone, revealing a splash of intrigue.

As a reminder, Val says, "I'll see you there."

"Uh, Val?"

"I promise to behave," Val says, and after a short pause, continues, "mostly." Val gives Charlene one more reassuring thumbs-up as she shooes her to the door.

As Charlene gingerly opens the door to greet Allen for their date, a cascade of anticipation rushes through her. Her heart flutters like an overexcited butterfly, and she takes a moment to be sure her hair is just right. The door swings open, revealing a beaming Allen, his face lighting up like a jackpot winner in a casino. Their eyes lock, and a burst of nervous laughter escapes Charlene's lips.

Allen's blue shirt and black jacket somehow intensify the striking depth of his blue eyes. Charlene can't help but think, "A girl could get lost in those eyes, and be perfectly fine with it." They're the kind of eyes that feel like endless oceans, mysterious, magnetic, and just dangerous enough that she half expects to need a lifeboat and a compass, but wouldn't mind sinking anyway. Her stomach flips, her cheeks warm, and she quickly looks away—because if she stares a second longer, she might actually forget how to breathe.

Allen is momentarily spellbound by Charlene's beauty—an

almost otherworldly radiance, with hair pinned up just enough to let silken ringlets tumble around her face, catching the light as though each curl held a secret shimmer meant only for him. The beautiful, radiant, black pleated metallic lamé dress shimmers like liquid midnight as it flows over her every curve with soft, mesmerizing elegance.

Recalling her manners, Charlene introduces Allen and Val with a touch of formality. "Allen, this is my best friend-"

"-and stylist," Val interjected proudly.

"Val."

Val doesn't waste a moment and playfully greets Allen with a simple, "Enchanted."

Charlene does a double-take, looking at Val, "Enchanted, Val? Really?" Charlene asks. "What country are we in? Just now, I forgot."

Val gives Charlene a blushing smile and shrugs, darting her eyes toward Allen. Allen chuckles.

Charlene and Allen turn to leave.

As Charlene turns to lock the door behind her, she waves privately at Val, who is very excited for her, almost jumping, and gives her the thumbs up.

"Go on. And, tell me everything tomorrow. I want to know everything. All the dirty little details," she says, giving Charlene a wink.

A tranquil hush envelopes the car as Allen and Charlene exchange only a few sparse words.

Allen compliments Charlene on her appearance, "You look amazing."

They gaze at each other.

"Thank you. So do you," responds Charlene, blushing just a little.

"You know, outside of work, I don't get out much."

Charlene figures that Allen's dance style must be hilariously stiff, his movements jerky and mechanical, as if he's trying to follow the beat but can't quite escape his robotic rhythm.

"You don't say," Charlene says as if it is the most unbelievable thing she has heard in a while.

"And so, I want to shake things up, you know? I've got a lot of fun to catch up on."

Chapter 9

Allen and Charlene arrive at CroonEoke's. They can feel the pulsation of the music as they open the door. The bump, bump, bump of the loud music seems to blow their hair back. Upon entering, they are immediately enveloped in a vibrant atmosphere. The infectious rhythm of swing music fills the air, pulsating through their bodies. The dance floor is alive with couples moving in sync, their bodies effortlessly swaying to the beat.

Laughter and chatter mingle with the music, creating a lively buzz. They are greeted by a rush of energy as they take in the sights and sounds of the swinging scene. There are couples engaged in dancing and partying, exhibiting uninhibited behavior with each other and other individuals present. Charlene catches sight of a couple of women in the far corner, noticing Allen, one an attractive redhead in a black mini dress and transparent blouse, and the other a brunette in a denim jean jumpsuit. The brunette catches Charlene's gaze and motions to Allen as if to ask, "Is this your guy?"

Not knowing exactly how to respond, Charlene just smiles back.

Charlene quietly reminds herself to keep things professional. But just as she's trying to maintain her cool composure, Allen grabs her hand like a daring pirate seizing his treasure and whisks her away to the dance floor, with her curls bouncing behind her. The two young ladies left behind exchange curious glances, soon joined by two men, sparking an unexpectedly lively and intriguing conversation.

Allen is a little stiff at first, dancing with almost jerky movements, but with a little coaxing from Charlene, he soon begins to loosen up. Allen and Charlene enthusiastically embrace the wild party atmosphere, immersing themselves in the energetic revelry and joining in on the uninhibited dancing, laughter, and merriment.

At first, Allen's dance moves seem to flow somewhere between robot and chicken, with the chicken part being his go-to, but he improves over a short time.

"You told me you don't get out much," Charlene shouts above the deafening music.

"I don't. But I do dance sometimes," Allen says.

They enthusiastically perform a series of silly dances on the dance floor, captivating everyone present. Their movements are playful and lighthearted, filled with an infectious energy that spreads throughout the room. With each step, they effortlessly transition from one comical dance move to another, showcasing their creativity and spontaneity. Their synchronized twirls, exaggerated spins, and comical facial expressions elicit laughter and applause from the onlookers. The couple's uninhibited enjoyment and carefree spirit were evident in their every gesture, creating a joyous atmosphere that made it impossible for anyone to resist joining in on the fun.

On the dance floor, Charlene and Allen are like mad scientists of movement, concocting a dance repertoire that defies convention and begs for a new page in the history of dance.

First, there is the "Electric Shuffle" – a series of rapid, synchronized shimmies that seem to channel the energy of a lightning storm. Then they do the "Funky Robot Waltz," a fusion of mechanical precision and groovy sway that leaves on-lookers both puzzled and captivated. They seamlessly transition into the "Spaghetti Limb Samba," limbs flailing and twirling like cooked noodles in a wild carnival of motion.

Their dance experimentations are a sight to behold, filled with wild abandon and infectious laughter.

The "Bungee Bop" had them bouncing and rebounding like they were attached to invisible elastic cords.

But perhaps the pièce de résistance is when Charlene and Allen invent the "Interstellar Slide," a cosmic fusion of gliding moonwalks and space-age arm extensions, transporting them to a celestial disco where stars are the dance partners.

In a spontaneous twirl, Charlene suddenly spots Val dancing with a buff young man who is also a regular at the club and a big fan of Val's. They are performing a hilarious dance routine that seems like a mash-up of caffeinated flamingos attempting the moonwalk while wearing clown shoes. Val waves excitedly at Charlene with both hands and a big grin. She's wearing an extravagant shimmery blue party dress with an all-over fringe trim, long gloves, and a tiara. She gives Charlene the thumbs up and continues dancing.

Through nods, facial expressions, and hand gestures, Val and Charlene communicate back and forth as if it's part of their dance. And they both burst out laughing. Val reassures Charlene that she will not tell Allen anything about Charlene's journalism profession and that she'll keep it secret. Charlene roughly gestures back a thank you. They continue to dance.

After a moment, Val gives Charlene a funny look.

"What?" Charlene ponders.

Val is mouthing a message to Charlene, but Charlene doesn't get it.

Suddenly, Val unleashes her battle cry, "Get 'em, girl!" as the music goes on an unexpected coffee break, leaving her proclamation hanging in the air like a confetti-filled piñata waiting for a whack. It turns out her exclamation is like a cherry on the excitement sundae, and the room erupts in a collective scream of delight.

Val and Charlene's epic laughter is drowned out by the music, which has now returned, and each returns to dancing with their partners.

As the night wears on, Allen and Charlene continue to unveil their dance creations, drawing in a crowd of intrigued onlookers who can't help but join in the chaotic, joyous fun. Their inventive dance floor experiments, full of arms flailing and hips twisting, were a testament to their willingness to defy convention and embrace the sheer delight of movement.

"You're a wonderful dancer," says Charlene.

Allen laughs, "You, too," and he gives Charlene a quick spin.

By the end of the night, they have not only danced their hearts out but also inspired a new wave of dance enthusiasts who can't wait to invent their own moves. Allen and Charlene may not have rewritten the dance history books, but they have certainly etched their names in the annals of dance floor legends, forever remembered as the pioneers of the delightfully unconventional.

After their whimsically eccentric dance, Charlene and Allen, still a little out of breath, plop down next to each other. The memory of their footwork faux pas and impromptu twirls, still fresh, prompts them to break into spontaneous laughter, each chuckle serving as an unspoken testament to their shared, delightful misadventure. Their eyes twinkle with mirth, shoulders shaking in harmony, the joy of their shared moment echoing around them. The dance may not have been perfect, but the shared laughter was priceless.

"Well, I think I've officially redefined the term 'two left feet,'" Allen joked.

Charlene laughs, "You weren't that bad. I mean, if the goal was to impersonate a malfunctioning robot, you nailed it-"

Suddenly, a man strides up to Charlene and asks her to dance. He is plainly dressed and has a 5 o'clock shadow. Not wanting to separate from Allen, she hesitates but reluctantly agrees, all while keeping a careful eye on Allen. Meanwhile, another man approaches Allen, dramatically pretending to recognize him from the movies. He is wearing a plaid shirt and black denim jeans. Without warning, he rolls up his sleeves and challenges Allen to an arm-wrestling match, slurring something about proving his strength against a "movie star." Allen tries to decline, but the man is insistent, so with a sigh and a shrug, Allen agrees.

The match is over in seconds, with Allen easily pinning the man's arm to the table. The challenger, not one to admit defeat, blames his loss on being "a little too drunk to wrestle properly" before stumbling away.

Now alone at the table, Allen's eyes drift back to Charlene on the dance floor. But before he can even think about joining her, two strikingly attractive women appear at his side, each vying for his attention. One tosses her hair, the other leans in with a playful laugh, and Allen is left awkwardly juggling compliments and glances toward the dance floor, wishing he could escape the sudden spotlight.

"Excuse me, ladies," Allen says politely as he shifts from

between the two women and makes his way back onto the dance floor.

The man Charlene is dancing with starts to move in a way that feels a bit too suggestive, making her increasingly uncomfortable. She glances back toward the table, hoping to find Allen, but he's nowhere in sight. A flicker of panic sets in as she considers how to extract herself gracefully.

Just as the discomfort begins to peak, she feels the gentle touch of a familiar hand slipping into hers—it's Allen. He's come to her rescue. With easy confidence, he guides her away from her overly forward dance partner, offering a polite but firm nod in the man's direction.

"Mind if I cut in?" Allen says, his tone calm but with just enough edge to leave no room for argument.

As Charlene steps into Allen's arms, relief washes over her, and for the first time that evening, she feels completely at ease. The tension melts away, replaced by a new, unexpected energy as they move together on the dance floor.

The two women huff in frustration from the corner, their carefully laid plan completely foiled.

As they notice the night drawing to a close, Allen and Charlene once again go to the dance floor. They share a slow dance during the evening's final song. Even though the beat is still lively, they sway together in a slow dance, their hair slightly tousled and clothes a bit disheveled from the night's festivities. They gracefully move across the dance floor, their bodies swaying in perfect harmony. With each step, their movements are intentional. Their feet glide across the polished surface, creating a mesmerizing rhythm. As they dance, their bodies remain close, their arms wrapped around each other, creating a sense of intimacy and connection. The couple seems lost in their own world, their eyes locked on each other, holding each other close, oblivious to the surrounding crowd. Charlene wonders whether a connection is developing between them. Charlene again dismisses the idea of a potential connection with Allen, assuming he is involved with Gina. And of course, she is not one to want to break up a pair. Allen and Charlene dance gracefully to the last lively swing music songs of the night.

Noticing her faraway expression, Allen gracefully spins Charlene on the dance floor, hoping to ignite a radiant smile on her face. Anytime Charlene appears lost in her thoughts, Allen spins her around, hoping to coax a smile from her lips, which works every time. Allen spins her once more toward the door, and they leave the nightclub with a stylish flourish, which is not missed by Val.

Charlene is feeling slightly sentimental as Allen drops her off at her home's door. They laugh together as they recount the night's events. They stand at the door, feeling that the atmosphere has suddenly become saturated with a touch of romance as if the universe itself conspired to set the stage for an enchanting interlude. Charlene wants to kiss him, but once again, she recalls Gina. Politely, Charlene and Allen kiss each other on the cheek, then they pause and smile at each other, their eyes meeting, still somewhat breathless from all the night's dancing.

Charlene thinks now is the perfect moment to ask, "Are you seeing – "

"I had a good time with you tonight."

Charlene nearly invites Allen in for coffee. However, her hopes are quickly dashed when he promptly takes her hand, kisses it, thanks her for the wonderful night, and turns to walk back to his car.

"All the better," she thinks. She realizes that Clay is right, she is getting a bit too close. "A bit," she thinks. As she is slowly closing the door behind her. She can't help but wonder if this is the end of their evening together.

She feels uncertain as she contemplates whether he holds any romantic interest in her, "or..." She dismisses the thought, reluctant to entertain it further. After all, there's Gina to consider. She pauses quietly, reminding herself of her real purpose, and that's getting the news story. What about the story? Or is there a story to be had?

Suddenly, Allen surprises her by quickly turning and asking, "How about a jog tomorrow?"

She spins to face him, almost throwing herself off-balance but trying not to seem desperate. "Sure," she responds.

He takes a moment, grins, and utters, "Alright, I'll swing by at the crack of dawn, 7:00 AM sharp." With that, he hops into his trusty vehicle – a surprisingly unassuming but reliable midsize car with tinted windows, and zooms away.

Chapter 10

Charlene finds herself lost in thought tonight, her mind consumed by thoughts of Allen. As she lay in bed, she couldn't help but smile at the memories that flooded her mind. Suddenly, she stops herself, wondering what she is thinking. And why is she pining for him? Despite her confusion, she can't shake the feeling that something is missing without him by her side.

That morning, Allen shows up at Charlene's doorstep, ready for their morning jog.

Hoping to exude elegance and suavity, Charlene hollers to him, "Hey, Allen! Make yourself comfortable and come on in. Mi casa es su casa!" Little does he know, Charlene is inside, frantically trying to get dressed without tripping over her own shoelaces.

Kicking off his running shoes, Allen prepares to enter. Charlene's comfortable, quiet home interior welcomes Allen as he steps inside. Allen notices that the color palette in her home predominantly features yellow, brass, and gold. The cozy tangerine-orange sofa invites him to sink into its plush cushions, exuding comfort. Nearby, the soft glow of a gold-plated brass table lamp casts a warm, welcoming ambiance. The mustard-colored walls and sandstone carpet tie the room together with earthy sophistication.

Allen's curiosity is piqued, and he finds himself wanting to learn more about Charlene. Casually, he starts to explore the surroundings. As Allen delves deeper into his exploration, he can't help but notice a tabletop adorned with well-worn books and novels, tempting him to immerse himself in their pages. Amid a tall stack of romance novels, he spots books on leadership, management, and professional development, offering insight into Charlene's interests and passions.

There are photos on the walls, the fireplace mantle, and tables throughout the room. One photo shows Charlene as a child in a blue jumper. There is a colorful toy train set on the floor next to her, with bright red, blue, and yellow train cars. A stack of picture books is visible on a nearby shelf, showcasing various fairy tales and adventure stories. A small stuffed teddy bear sits on a chair in the background, its worn fur indicating years of love and companionship. The room is well-lit, with sunlight streaming in through a large window, casting a warm glow on Charlene's smiling face. "Who is this person in the light blue jumper?"

"That's me as a wee one!" she shouts from her bedroom. "I was basically a pint-sized newshound. Even my teddy bears couldn't escape my breaking news updates! But enough about that... I'll leave the rest to your imagination," Charlene quips, stopping short of spilling all the childhood beans.

In another picture, he sees a little girl with wispy reddish-gold hair. Alongside her is a large, colorful lollipop, and sticky candy is on her face. In the background, balloons of various shapes and sizes add to the whimsical atmosphere. Additionally, a small puppy is jumping up toward the girl, trying to catch the lollipop. The girl's hair is so wispy that it seems to float around her head, creating a comical contrast to her serious expression. Overall, the picture captures a playful and lighthearted moment that brings a smile to his face.

"And this one with the puppy?"

"That's my little sister, Kim, and our puppy, Goober. We nicknamed them the messy duo. Wherever there was a mess, they were always close by."

Allen chuckles. On a nearby shelf, Allen sees a photo of Charlene and her mother. He smiles. It's like they were cut from the same genetic cookie dough, with Charlene being the freshly baked version of her mom. They share the same uncanny ability to give the "mom look" that can make anyone instantly reconsider their life choices. It's like a hereditary superpower that Charlene's been using since birth! "You look just like your mom," Allen calls out. "Carbon copy. Well, I know what you're going to look like when you're older – exactly the same! You don't age."

Next to these pictures are a series of images depicting Charlene's accomplishments. Each picture shows a clear progression, highlighting her activities and achievements.

One picture captures Charlene as a young teenager in a leotard standing on a high school stage. The teenager is striking a pose, showcasing her flexibility and grace.

"Here's a picture of you in a leotard..."

"That picture's from my high school performance."

"Were you any good?"

"Yes. I was a pretty good dancer."

"Yeah?"

"Well, mostly. I fell off the stage once."

Another picture captures Charlene as a teenager at her graduation, a milestone moment in her life. She stands tall in her graduation gown, tossing her cap into the air, radiating confidence and pride. Her smile is infectious, reflecting the years of hard work and dedication that led her to this achievement. In her hand, she holds her diploma, a tangible symbol of her academic success. The picture captures a moment of triumph and the beginning of a new chapter in her life.

Allen transitions from one photograph to another, recounting with a chuckle, "Ah, your high school graduation... and here you are, caught napping in college on a desk next to a toppled coffee mug... but it's crystal clear you love your coffee."

"Absolutely. It's a must-have every morning," Charlene responds with a chuckle.

However, as she's about to put on her gym shoes, Charlene suddenly remembers some items on a bookshelf that she can't afford to expose, as revealing them would jeopardize her cover. Her cherished CandidExposé employee badge is openly visible. A hushed gasp escapes her lips as she rushes to the bedroom door and sees Allen start to make his way towards the bookshelf. Charlene rushes into the room, her shoelaces tripping her, but she quickly recovers. She swiftly and discreetly tucks the badge away behind a nearby photograph.

Allen finds her behavior a little odd but chuckles and tells her, "You know, there's no rush. The fitness trail will still be there."

Charlene laughs and relaxes. "Yes. Sounds good. I am raring to go."

Arriving at Allen's beloved trail, they disembark from his car. As Charlene sets her sights on the trail head, a stark realization dawns upon her – it's been quite a while since she last went jogging, perhaps just a brief trip to the corner store last Wednesday. "That's quite the lengthy trail," she says comically as she admires the scenic expanse of nature before her.

"Yeah, it's my favorite trail. This is where I've done my fastest

100-meter sprint – 18 seconds!"

Charlene is impressed. In her strategic wisdom, she deduces that the present moment is ripe for some insightful inquiries. She begins asking Allen what-if type questions.

She formulates a question testing the waters to see if he considers himself single: "What if your significant other planned a surprise for you—what kind of surprise would you love?"

"I don't know."

"What if you had a plus-one to a wedding tomorrow—who would you bring?"

"Where are we going with this?"

She realizes that she is not necessarily asking him questions for public consumption; she just wants to know personally, but he seems to cringe at some of her questions. She is beginning to think maybe her line of questioning is a little too personal. But what other way is there to find the answers than to ask with utmost sincerity? "I want to know, are you seeing anyone?" she blurts.

Allen's eyes begin to sparkle as he gives a knowing smile. "All you have to do is ask. Now, was that so hard?"

"No, it wasn't so hard," Charlene replies, realizing that he didn't answer her question.

"Ok. So, I'll pick you up tomorrow morning for our jog."

Chapter 11

After stretching, Charlene and Allen begin their jog. After some time, they find themselves on a picturesque bridge that seems straight out of a fairy tale. The soft, mellow light of the setting sun bathes everything in a warm, golden glow. Beneath the bridge, a gentle stream meanders, its soothing gurgles creating a tranquil symphony that blends seamlessly with the rustling leaves and distant bird calls, beckoning them to be part of the moment.

They stand together, side by side, in a comfortable silence, as the sounds of nature envelop them in a soft embrace.

In that moment, everything else melts into the background, leaving just the two of them enveloped in the tranquility of the scene. It's a snapshot of an unadulterated, unspoken connection, where words become superfluous, and the surrounding beauty communicates volumes. Charlene turns towards Allen, her gaze earnest as she poses a heartfelt question, inquiring, "Why are you so distant? Why don't you share your thoughts?"

"What do you mean?"

"You know, when you are in public, you never interview."

"I like my privacy," Allen explains. "Plus, it keeps everybody on their toes when I take off."

They both laugh, and the realization comes over them both

that they are friends now, maybe more.

That evening, while in the van, Clay informs Charlene that he found something in their old footage. The video footage shows Gina and Allen sharing a long kiss as if they stepped right into the heart of an old romantic movie before Gina gets into her limousine and drives away.

Charlene's immediate reaction is, "Okay, yeah, that's not much," but listening to Clay's excitement, Charlene figures that's it - it's over. Whatever she had imagined could have been with Allen, she had to let it go. The story must go on.

Clay's comment doesn't help much when he says simply, "Yeah, a kiss like that, there's got to be something there."

The next day at the office, Charlene is in full-on unease mode. She whips out the video evidence of Allen and Gina locking lips and presents it to Horace. But as he squints at the screen, she can't help but wonder if it'll do the trick or if he's just going to be like, "Is that them smooching or a blurry UFO sighting?" The doubt's eating at her like a squirrel at a bird feeder, making her question if this scandalous kiss cam will make the cut for the evening news.

Without missing a beat, Horace swiftly responds, "Okay, they're kissing – and that's not even square-on. So, yeah, that's not much. And so, you got bupkis."

Charlene froze, her lips pressing into a thin line as Horace's comment echoed in her mind. Her eyes darted back to the image, focusing on the kiss with a sharper gaze.

Her brow furrows as thoughts begin to shift in her mind: "That wasn't passion—it was precision. Too precise. Like it was staged? Hmm. What's really going on here?"

Horace continues, and he is impatient. "Come on, Charlene, you've got to give us the juice. Where's the juice you gave us before?"

Charlene's focus snaps back to Horace.

"Come on, I've given you great stories."

"Look, it's simple: Find out if he's serious with her. If he's serious with her, you've got a story. And if he's not, you've got a story. Maybe not as big, but it's still a story."

Val joins a few colleagues who are eavesdropping outside Horace's office. Val whispers to another employee, "But, if there's nothing there, does she really have a story?"

Horace needs more tantalizing news about Allen and his potential love interest with Gina, if that's what it is.

Horace's office door opens again, and the curious employees are now up and about, moving around the office, heading to the water cooler, and pretending to be working.

Charlene is back talking with Val in Val's cubicle; Val is now asking, "What is taking you so long to get the interview? What's the big deal? Zip, zip, and you're done."

"It's not that simple," says Charlene. "He's like a clam, all pinned up, and sealed with glue. I understand she's like that, too. It's like a secret agreement they have together—probably written in invisible ink. It may take a while."

"But there is something about this kiss – "

Clay strolls into the office, and, casually peeking in, asks, "What are we talking about?"

"Clay," Charlene says. She motions to herself and Val, and gently says, "Lady talk. Do you mind?"

Clay rolls his eyes, "You know, it might behoove you to include me in on some of your conversations more often, I am your cameraman, you know. And, every bit of information helps me, too," and moves on.

"He's right, you know," Val says, agreeing with Clay.

"That's right!" Clay's voice interjects from the other side of the cubicle wall.

Then, immediately, Val continues to the meat of their conversation, telling Charlene, "You're going to need to talk to Allen about the things that he likes to talk about and do."

"Uh, yeah? That's the job."

Clay peeks in again and asks, "Why don't you go and meet him on the set?"

"Great idea," Val says, "That way, you can get the whole scoop. When you go there, just be cool."

Just then, Horace steps into view, "You still here? Get out there and get that story." Then he walks away and down the hallway.

Charlene scoffs. Privately, she jests, "These cubicles should come with doors... and a ceiling."

Val chuckles, "Yeah, but they wouldn't be called cubicles. They would be offices, and we have plenty of those, right now."

The next day, Charlene uses her connections to get on set. Once inside, she cleverly utilizes her news reporter badge to gain access to restricted areas, flashing it like a badge of honor or a superhero cape. With her badge prominently displayed, she confidently approaches security checkpoints and presents it as proof of her authorized presence. With a confident smile, she gestures towards her badge, proudly displaying her name and affiliation. The privilege enables her to capture exclusive behind-the-scenes footage and conduct interviews with crucial personnel. Charlene's strategic use of her news reporter badge proves to be an invaluable tool in her pursuit of breaking news and in delivering accurate, timely reports to her audience.

Chapter 12

The movie set features the cityscape at night. The set crew is diligently working to bring the director's vision to life. They are setting up the various props and scenery, and carefully arranging each element to create the desired atmosphere. Lighting technicians are strategically positioning lights to enhance the mood and highlight the actors. Sound engineers test and adjust audio equipment to ensure clear, crisp sound quality. Camera operators are setting up their equipment and framing shots, capturing every scene with precision. Grips and electricians are busy rigging and securing equipment to ensure the safety of the cast and crew. Makeup artists and wardrobe stylists are meticulously preparing the actors to ensure they look their best on camera. The entire crew is working together seamlessly, each person playing a vital role in the production process. Their attention to detail and dedication to their craft are evident as they work tirelessly to create a captivating movie experience.

Charlene realizes she must interview Allen, but the daunting task of precisely how to broach the subject of Gina has yet to cross her mind. However, Charlene possesses a nimble mind, and she's confident that she'll devise an approach when the opportune moment presents itself.

Amidst the bustling film set, she presses on with her quest to locate Allen. A crew member points the way.

The movie set setting captivates the senses. The hammering on the scenery reverberates through the air, creating a cacophony of sharp, metallic clangs and resonating thuds. Each strike of the hammer produces a distinct sound, ranging from the high-pitched tinkling of metal on metal to the deep, hollow thumps as the hammer connects with the wooden framework. The rhythm of the hammering is relentless, punctuated by occasional pauses and followed by a flurry of rapid strikes. The noise echoes throughout the space, filling it with a symphony of mechanical percussion. Overall, the hammering creates a symphony of sound that is both chaotic and mesmerizing.

As the director's voice booms, "Quiet on the set!" an immediate silence falls over the entire set. The previously bustling, noisy environment abruptly transforms into a still, hushed atmosphere. All conversations cease, footsteps come to a halt, and even the sound of breathing seems to diminish.

The sudden absence of noise creates a palpable tension, as everyone on set eagerly awaits the next command. The silence is so profound that even the smallest sound, like a pin dropping, would be amplified. A cacophony of bangs persists for a brief moment until the director shoots a look that could curdle milk, at which point the noise abruptly surrenders as if it remembers it has dinner reservations elsewhere. It is a moment of anticipation and focus, as everyone prepares for the next scene to unfold.

Allen is getting ready to perform his stunts.

The director shouts, "Action!" Allen jumps from the roof of a building, landing on a pile of cardboard boxes. He runs through the streets, dodging obstacles and performing daring moves, his muscles tense and ready for action. He expertly dodges obstacles and realistic bricks being hurled at him, leaping over crates and sliding under pipes. His movements are fluid and precise, a testament to his years of training. As he runs, he performs daring moves, flipping over cars and scaling walls with ease. The crowd watches in awe as he blazes past, a blur of motion and adrenaline. The crew watches in awe as he finishes the scene flawlessly. Allen feels a rush of adrenaline and excitement as he takes off his safety gear. The director congratulates him on a job well done. Allen smiles, knowing that this is what he loves to do. He can't wait for the next scene.

As Charlene arrives on set, wondering how to uncover the answers she's seeking, she's brimming with eagerness to strike up a conversation with Allen. It isn't long before Charlene begins imagining their meeting..... Charlene imagines the perfect next encounter with Allen, on set, she envisions a serene, quiet setting—perhaps the hammering has stopped just for their encounter. And of course, there is a gentle breeze blowing through their hair. They're sitting on a park bench imported for the scene under a canopy of trees, also imported. The air feels light and easy, with a soft breeze from the giant fans on set, and the gentle sounds of nature in the background playing from sound devices, setting the ideal stage for an open, heart-to-heart conversation.

In her mind, Allen begins by looking at her with a sense of trust and vulnerability, as if he's ready to share everything. She imagines him starting slowly, cautiously, but with an honesty that makes her heart race a little. He begins to open up about his thoughts, feelings, and uncertainties, especially regarding relationships and life decisions. Then, Charlene seizes the moment and asks the question that's been on her mind: "Are you seeing Gina Tarvec?" All is quiet as Allen parts his lips to speak, and –

Feigning a cool conversation with Allen, she casually leans against a wooden prop wall with a faux-brick design, causing it to fall and suddenly snapping her out of her daydream. She scrambles to put the scenery wall back up before Allen arrives. She doesn't want him to see her making a mess of the movie set. She grabs a nearby hammer and nails and gets to work, her heart racing. The wall is heavy and awkward, but she manages to prop it up against the backdrop. Charlene struggles to lift the massive section of the movie set scenery wall into place. As she pushes against it, the wall suddenly leans back, sending her tumbling onto it and falling over like a banana peel. She clings to the wall, trying to steady it, but it is too heavy. With a loud crash, the wall collapses, sending debris flying everywhere. Charlene lay there, stunned. Then, Allen comes in. She looks up and sees him standing over her, "Hello," she says.

Allen's humorous reaction to discovering that Charlene has destroyed part of the set is nothing short of comical. With wide eyes and a dropped jaw, he let out an exaggerated gasp, as if he had just witnessed the most shocking event in history. Charlene looks hilarious as she is splayed across the scenery. Her limbs are sprawled in every direction, resembling a human pretzel. Her facial expression is a mix of surprise and bewilderment, as if she can't quite believe what has just happened. Her disheveled hair adds to the comical effect, sticking out in all directions like a wild bird's nest. It is a sight that can easily have been mistaken for a slapstick comedy skit. A burst of laughter escapes Allen's lips, followed by a playful shake of his head. He can't help but find the situation amusing, even though it means extra work to fix the damage. "Ok, no more coffee for you for a while," he says as he takes her hand to help her up.

The director sees the damage and shouts, "Allen! Get your fan off the set! Somebody, come and clean this mess up!" He walks off grumbling.

"Wow, is that all he's going to do? You must have a tranquilizing effect on people."

Moments later, they hear a loud door slam and the unmistakable sound of a piece of furniture crashing.

"Okay, there it is. That's the reaction I was expecting," Allen says, gesturing in the direction of the door slam.

Charlene is standing on the backdrop. Her hair is mussed as if she had just waltzed with a tornado. "Oops."

Chapter 13

It's evening, and Charlene is sitting in the van with Clay. Clay is laughing, finding humor in the fact that Charlene had destroyed the set. "What were you thinking? Ha haha! Well, what did Allen say?"

"He is actually quite understanding," Charlene says, trying to pull off an air of sophistication.

Clay continues laughing loudly.

"Shh-h, quiet, quiet, I think he's coming out, now," Charlene says.

Allen and Gina are standing in front of Allen's place, talking and holding hands. Charlene thinks that it looks like he is consoling her, but she can't be sure. Moments later, Allen looks up and notices the van. Charlene gasps and ducks down in the driver's seat, wondering if he saw her. Allen and Gina enter the house, and before turning away, he gives the van one more puzzled look as they go inside his place. Clay humorously says, "I don't think they saw you."

"One of us should go over there and look in the window," Charlene suggests.

"Yeah," Clay replies.

"Okay, yeah, let me know what you see," says Charlene.

"Me? No, you. You've got that one-of-a-kind charm, you

know, your gift of gab," Clay says.

"I've spoiled you, Clay," Charlene says, half-jokingly, before reluctantly climbing out of the van.

"Wait," calls Clay, "What are you going to say if they see you?"

"I'm going to say you made me do it," Charlene responds jokingly.

"Haw, haw," Clay gives a slow, fake laugh. "Oh sure, and I'll pretend you're some random stranger with your own set of problems."

Shaking her head and smiling, "Give me that," Charlene takes the video camera with her. She finds herself at Allen's door. Peeking in through the side window, she can see Allen and Gina standing in the living room, talking. Gina seems to be excited, jumping up and down. She hugs Allen, but Charlene can't make out what they're saying. Must be something really exciting. Like a proposal? Is he proposing?

Gina notices Charlene, who quickly ducks out of sight, and with a playful glint in her eye, pulls Allen in for a sudden hug and kiss, determined to give the nosy reporters something to talk about.

Quickly, Charlene films their embrace and the kiss. Charlene's mind races as she considers the potential consequences of Allen proposing to Gina. She can't help but wonder if their friendship would be irreparably damaged if Allen and Gina were to become engaged. Charlene realizes she has feelings for Allen, though she does not act on them, choosing instead to value their friendship above all else. The thought of losing that friendship is almost unbearable. She tries to push the thoughts from her mind, but they linger, leaving her anxious and unsettled. Only time will tell what the future holds for her and Allen's friendship. Charlene stands outside Allen's house, peering through the window of his front door, curious about his furniture and how he is living. It is different from the simple industrial style she expected: the interior design of his home is a wild fusion of testosterone and tropical flair, with a purple-painted coffee table, large colorful picture books, and this morning's protein drink. In the windows, bullet casings turned into curtain tiebacks, complementing silky lime-green curtains, hunter-green fabric wallpaper, beige furniture, and a huge ficus with a canopy that covers half the ceiling. Charlene slowly moves around to the side of Allen's home, where she can see more. Now, shin-deep in yellow mums, Charlene takes in more of Allen's home. The dining area has lime-green curtains, deep-blue and white-painted walls, and blue cushions in formal-looking wooden chairs. A rugged army green duffel rests by the door, hinting at his action-packed lifestyle. Allen himself—a man who thrives on adventure but appreciates balance and precision in his space. Charlene can't help but wonder what Allen's daily life is like, and what kind of person he is. She lingers for a moment longer.

Just then, Allen enters the room.

Quickly, she drops down into the shrubbery outside of Allen's window, and when the coast is clear, she promptly walks back to the van. "Let's go," she says as she turns the key in the ignition.

Allen's door opens, and he catches sight of the van just as they drive away. He's puzzled ,but he doesn't think much about it.

Chapter 14

The following day, Allen and Charlene meet up for lunch at a new cozy cafe. The cozy cafe exudes a warm and inviting ambiance. Soft, dim lighting creates a cozy atmosphere, while the gentle hum of conversation adds a comforting background noise.

As they sit down, Charlene begins to ask Allen more personal questions to break the ice, "What's the most romantic gesture someone has ever done for you—or that you've done for someone?"

"I don't know," Allen responds. "What is this, 21 questions?"

"Sure. Why not?"

Allen pauses to decide if he wants to answer Charlene's curious questions and says, "Ok, ok. But I'll need you to answer some questions, also, because I want to get to know about you."

"Ok." She wasn't expecting to get her answers this way, but she thought why not? If this is what it takes to get them, she is willing to partake. "Ok, sure," she says, thinking this was going to be just like a game of 21 questions.

"What's your favorite sandwich?" Allen asks.

And, so it begins with a little small talk and personal questions to get to know each other. "Sandwich? Really?" she asks. It was far from where she wanted to start the conversation.

"Yeah, sure."

"Okay. Cucumber, lettuce, and hummus....," Charlene says. Allen pretends to yawn.

"With micro greens," Charlene continues.

"Okay, that sounds good. Throw in some red peppers, and we're talking."

"Alright. What is your favorite place on earth?" Charlene asks.

"Big Sur, California. I like the Mediterranean feel. And yours?"

"Key West, Florida," says Charlene.

"What's there?"

"A whole chain of islands hanging off the southern coast of Florida. It's like experiencing the Caribbean without actually leaving the continental U.S.," says Charlene.

Allen smiles, thinking she sounds like a television commercial. "What is this, an ad? Now you want me to fly to Key West? You're going to make me want to fly there. I will take a plane, right now, and fly there. And you'd have to come with me. You could be like my tour guide."

Charlene laughs. "Why not?"

"Yeah," Allen smirks, "Well, what do you like to do?"

Charlene smiles and responds, "I like sleeping in late, and uh, reading the latest celebrity news drama. ...And, sleeping in general."

"I thought you were going to say you like drinking overpriced lattes in the morning," laughs Allen.

"What? Why?"

"Pardon me. I don't mean to be assuming, but, you seem to be the type, you know, someone who appreciates the experience and atmosphere of a trendy café. A real city-dweller, creative professional, someone who enjoys socializing in chic, cozy environments."

Caught off guard by how accurately he described her, she didn't want to appear too predictable. "Well, no. Maybe just a coffee," Charlene replied.

"You like drinking overpriced coffee?" asks Allen, leaning in with a smile.

"No, just coffee."

"Tea for me," says Allen. "I like sampling the aroma first and then tasting a sip on my palate. I consider myself a bit of a connoisseur," he states with his chin up and an air of pride.

"Really?" Charlene smiles, thinking of the many times she's asked her interviewees to "spill the tea."

"Yes," Allen says, smiling.

"What is the last book you read?"

"A book by the magician Troy Lafontaine called Wacky Wizardry."

"Ah, Wacky Wizardry," recalls Charlene. "I've heard of it. How is it?"

Allen scratches his head, trying to recollect a bizarre story he had just devoured from the magician's book. With a grin, he begins to recount one in all its hilarious glory:

"Apparently, there was a magician who could only make inanimate objects disappear. His greatest trick was making a garden gnome vanish, but then he couldn't find it, so his wife made him sleep in the doghouse. Literally. He accidentally made himself disappear, too. The moral of the story? Don't mess with the wife's garden gnomes!" Allen chuckles, shaking his head at the collection of whimsical tales he had encountered in Wacky Wizardry. "How about you?"

"I am reading the book, Aurora Bonneville," replies Charlene excitedly. "It's a story about a young woman on a remarkable journey to run a farm all on her own."

"A farm, huh?"

"Yes."

"Bet there are no action scenes in the book."

"No, not so far. Just a bit of milking, mucking, and making hay with the farm hands," Charlene responds, smiling. "Tell me about your family," she asks.

Allen hesitates, sensing a twinge of being put under the spotlight as if he's amid an impromptu interrogation. "Yeah, it's just my brother and me. We were raised by wolves. Grey wolves." He pauses, watching for Charlene's reaction. And then, seeing her wide-eyed, incredulous expression, he bursts out laughing. "I'm kidding. I come from a small family. Just my mom, dad, and younger brother. Grew up in a typical small town."

"What about your childhood?"

"What is there to say? I was a kid."

"Something had to draw you into acting. What was it?"

"I saw a movie with my favorite action star, Bill Payne. He did his own stunts, taking on all the action scenes. That was really him in every scene. He was great," Allen says with stars in his eyes. "It was then that I knew I had to do it, too. I had to become an action star."

"Bill Payne, star of Runaway Flight: Can't Catch Me?" Charlene asks. "Um, that movie –"

"That movie only got 2 stars, I know," says Allen, "but the actor was great."

Feeling a moment of warmth, Charlene attempts to ask a more profound question: "If you could date any celebrity, who would it be?"

But Allen deflects with a teasing grin, "Honestly, I think I'd just end up in a tabloid for crashing their red carpet event. Besides, I'm much better off with someone who doesn't have a team of stylists."

Charlene notices that, with her line of questioning, he still hasn't let on whether he is seeing anyone. Although she can feel she is getting closer to the answer, she senses tension from Allen, so she opts for different non-relationship-related questions. They play for a while longer, continuing to laugh and joke. They find it humorous when they finish each other's sentences.

Chapter 15

C harlene uses her badge to get on set again. A romantic setting for his movie, the setting is the billionaire's backyard scene, is a picturesque garden filled with vibrant hues of purple and gold, with tropical flowers and topiaries. The garden features a charming gazebo adorned with delicate slowly twinkling bright, white fairy lights, creating a magical ambiance. A meandering stone pathway leads to a tranquil pond, where a graceful fountain gently sprays water into the air. The setting is complete with a breathtaking sunset that paints the sky with hues of pink, orange, and gold, casting a warm glow over the entire scene.

The director looks up and sees Charlene peering in through a doorway. "Hey!" the director calls out to her.

"Oh! Caught me," Charlene thinks, wincing.

"What are you doing here!?!" the director screams. "You need to go. It took us four hours to put that last set back together."

Charlene assures the director, "I promise I won't go anywhere near the set. I just want to watch Allen in action."

After a brief back-and-forth — and some careful explaining — he hesitates. Whether it's her persistence or the reminder that she's there to interview Allen, he finally relents.

"Alright," after a few moments, he finally agrees. "Don't

touch anything!"

"Nothing," Charlene agrees.

"Nothing!" he emphasizes boldly.

"Nothing," she softly assures.

The director resigns his stance and slaps his head, "Eddie!" he calls to his assistant, determined to be ready for anything. "Get me the wood glue... and my aspirin!"

Charlene watches Allen's performance silently, certain not to touch anything, as promised. Allen's character has collected the item, a set of government secrets, and is escaping from the back of the billionaire's mansion. His action scene showcases a thrilling array of daring stunts as he fearlessly leaps, flips, and battles through the chaos. He swiftly navigates the obstacles, expertly navigating the dangerous scene and skillfully avoiding several random explosions that erupt around him, showcasing his impressive athleticism. As the tension escalates, Allen's determination is evident in his every move. A group of menacing ruffians surrounds him, their rough appearance and aggressive postures creating an intimidating atmosphere. They are demanding a high-stakes ransom from Allen, believing he possesses a valuable secret that the billionaire has hidden, and they want him to hand it over. Their motivations are fueled by greed and desperation, and they're willing to resort to intimidation to get what they want. The tension in the air is palpable as they close in on him. Now, they've just about got him cornered. Their eyes are filled with malice. The actor's heart races as he assesses the situation, searching for a way to escape the impending danger. In a swift and calculated motion, Allen skillfully evades a barrage of bullets, his reflexes honed to perfection. With precision and agility, he executes a final air kick, his leg extending gracefully through the air, defeating his adversaries. Allen finishes an acting scene by swinging on a rope, landing on a platform, and grabbing his leading lady by the waist, shouting," Paula!"

Charlene imagines herself as the leading lady in the scene.... She envisions Allen finishing his action-packed moment by swinging effortlessly on a rope and landing gracefully on a platform next to her. In her mind, he pulls her into his arms, grabs her by the waist with a charming grin, and shouts, "Paula!" The rush of excitement floods through her as she imagines the chemistry between them sparking like fireworks on screen. But her daydream shatters when she's jolted back to reality by the actress's voice: "Biff!" she cries out, tears glistening in her eyes. "Thank you. You've rescued me once again."

"I had to. I wasn't going to leave you there surrounded by explosives and bullets flying everywhere. You can't run that fast. I had to make sure you're safe."

"You're my hero," she says, and she gives Allen a long kiss.

They stand together, a striking image, with Allen holding onto the rope with one hand while his arm wraps around her waist. Her long, hair blows gracefully in the breeze.

"Cut!" the director yells. "Excellent work! And that is a wrap!"

Among the bustle of their surroundings, the actors congratulate one another.

"Good work," the leading lady tells Allen. "Makeup!" she squawks to the crew and walks off.

The appreciative applause from everyone on the movie set is thunderous, echoing throughout the sound stage and filling the air with palpable energy. It is a moment of collective celebration and recognition for the hard work and talent that went into the production. The clapping hands and enthusiastic cheers were a testament to the exceptional performances, the meticulous craftsmanship, and the seamless collaboration that had brought the film to life. The applause reverberated in the hearts of everyone present, including her own, a lasting memory of a job well done. Charlene's initial skepticism towards Allen's acting has transformed into genuine appreciation. She now recognizes his talent and the effort he puts into his performances.

Charlene meets Allen after the scene. She catches herself, subduing her excitement, trying not to gush like a schoolgirl. "Wonderful work," she says sincerely.

"You really think so?"

"Absolutely. Excellent scene. And so romantic at the end. I have a newfound appreciation for your work."

With a warm smile that reaches his eyes, he says, "Just give me a moment to clean up," his voice carrying a hint of pleased surprise, as though realizing, perhaps for the first time, how much she values the things he does.

Allen walks Charlene to his dressing room, saying, "Wait here." He grabs a robe and leaves the room.

In a matter of seconds, curiosity gets the better of Charlene, and she begins to casually snoop around, looking through fun and flirty pictures and admiring personal messages from fans.

Allen's dressing room is a well-appointed space that reflects his status as both an actor and an action star. The room is adorned with tasteful decor, including framed movie posters and awards he has received throughout his career. She looks at each one individually. In the collection was an award recognizing excellence in cinematic achievements, including acting, and several recognitions for stunt work, honoring stunt performers in film and television.

As Charlene's gaze sweeps across the collection of movie

posters featuring actor Allen Howser, a wave of nostalgia and intrigue washes over her. Each poster seems to tell a story, not just about the party of the characters he portrays but about his journey in cinema.

The posters on the walls capture moments frozen in time, and as Charlene studies them, she feels as though she is peering into different worlds. In one, he stands as a dashing hero, his eyes filled with determination and courage as a great explosion occurs behind him. In another, he is the enigmatic figure, shrouded in mystery and intrigue, leaping a broken bridge over alligators below. The posters span genres, from heartwarming comedies to gripping dramas, and each reveals a different facet of Allen's acting prowess. She finds herself getting lost in the details – the way his expressions change, the emotions he conveys with a simple look, and the range of characters he brings to life, from soft to intense. It is like a gallery of personalities, all connected by the thread of Allen's talent.

Amidst the movie's magic, Charlene can't help but admire the dedication and passion that must have gone into each role. She imagines the countless hours of rehearsal, the challenges overcome, and the moments of pure joy that came from creating something memorable.

As she continues to gaze at the posters, she feels a growing sense of connection with Allen – not just as the actor, but as the person behind the characters. Each poster is a testament to his artistry and his ability to transform and transport audiences into different worlds.

In that moment, surrounded by the many visual snapshots of Allen's cinematic journey, Charlene feels a newfound appreciation for the depth and complexity of his craft. As Charlene peruses the nostalgic posters and memorabilia, she feels a twinge of reluctance. She knows she can't afford to get too caught up in nostalgia; there is important information she needs to uncover.

Allen's wardrobe cabinet is a stylish and meticulously organized treasure trove that would impress any fashion designer. It's a fashion organization that could rival a supermodel's Instagram feed.

"Wow, he's got quite the wardrobe," Charlene observes, her mind twirling through the possibilities as she contemplates which jackets she can elegantly experiment with.

Charlene continues her investigation. In a drawer of a small table by the door, Charlene finds a collection of friendly pictures; one stands out as a loving snapshot of Allen and Gina, captured in a humorous moment at a costume party. Allen is dressed in a white business shirt and sunglasses, while Gina is dressed as a beer maiden with big hair, a frilly white top, and an apron. They are holding each other in a warm embrace, faces pressed together, cheek-to-cheek, and a mixture of surprise and delight is evident in their expressions. Allen's sunglasses are slightly askew, giving him a comical appearance. Gina's hair is disheveled as if they had just been caught in the act of hugging. The picture captures the absurdity of the moment as if they were two unlikely characters caught in a hilarious sitcom scene. The sheer joy and unexpectedness of their embrace make this picture a delightful and lighthearted moment frozen in time.

As Charlene's curiosity gets the best of her, she decides to peek inside Allen's drawer. She quickly finds herself surrounded by a hushed atmosphere of anticipation. She slips two fingers in and slides the drawer open, her eyes scanning the contents within. There are a few bills and some admiring fan letters. But just as she is about to delve deeper, a faint sound reaches her ears – the telltale sound of the shower room door closing.

Panic set in as Charlene's heart skips a beat. With a sudden burst of realization, she swiftly withdraws her hand, her movements abrupt and almost comical in their haste. The expression on her face shifts from intrigue to mild panic as she processes the proximity of Allen's return from the shower area next door. With a flicker of desperation, she hurriedly places the pictures back in the drawer, and just as the dressing room door opens, she plunges into a nearby chair. Her face is the picture of casual nonchalance; she hopes beyond hope that her abrupt retreat from the drawer hasn't been too conspicuous, even though her heart is still racing from the adrenaline of her near-snooping escapade

Charlene prepares to greet him with a smile that she hopes is convincing enough to mask her guilt. It was a close call – one that would forever serve as a reminder that curiosity could be both a tantalizing and treacherous trait.

As Allen enters the room, fresh from his shower, half wrapped in his towel, and drying his hair with the other half, beads of water glisten on his skin in the soft light. Charlene's gaze wanders, drawn irresistibly toward Allen, who stands just a few steps away.

Allen is shirtless, wearing a pair of soft, comfortable-fitting jeans, seemingly unaware of the effect he is having on Charlene.

A soft warmth creeps into her cheeks, betraying the subtle flush that is rising in response to the unexpected sight before her. She quickly averts her gaze, hoping to maintain some semblance of composure despite the flurry of emotions stirring within her.

In that brief moment, as she feels the pull of her own thoughts and the undeniable presence of the shirtless Allen, Charlene finds herself grappling with a mixture of feelings. It is a mixture of appreciation for his form, surprise at the unexpected encounter, and a twinge of self-consciousness for her own reactions.

Charlene feels a rush of warmth flood her cheeks, but she can't look away. There's an undeniable magnetism in the way he stands before her, confidence radiating from every inch of his frame. Her heart races as he casually leans against the doorframe, his body relaxed yet undeniably alluring. He fixes her with a slow, gentle smile—a smile that feels like a secret invitation—and her breath catches in her throat. The intensity in his gaze pulls her in, making the air between them feel charged as if it's alive with unspoken possibilities. Before she realizes it, she's standing beside him, drawn in by the magnetic pull of his presence. "Hey there, lady," he continues, his voice low and teasing. "What are you up to?"

"I, um..." she stammers, struggling to regain her composure. Her mind racing with thoughts she had kept buried, desires she hadn't fully acknowledged until this very moment.

As if sensing the shift in the air, Allen steps closer, the towel shifting slightly, revealing more of his toned physique. As Allen's hand finds its place on her waist, his touch is firm yet gentle, sending a thrilling warmth through Charlene's entire body. He draws her closer, their breaths mingling in the charged space between them. His eyes, smoldering with intent, lock onto hers as his voice drops to a sultry whisper.

"I've been wondering how your lips would taste," he murmurs, his thumb grazing the curve of her hip, his grip steady yet full of unspoken promise. "And now that I have you this close, I don't think I can wait any longer to find out."

The words linger in the air like a spark, igniting the space between them as he leans in, his forehead brushing lightly against hers. His fingers tighten slightly on her waist, anchoring her to the moment as the rest of the world fades into the background.

Her breath catches, and the only answer she can give is the soft tilt of her chin, closing the gap that separates them from the inevitable—

A knock at the door interrupts the moment, as a stagehand calls out, "Everybody's leaving out. Will you close up, Allen?"

Allen clears his throat. "Yes, of course," he sighs, taking a moment to steady himself. What's the gentlemanly thing to do? The thought lingers as he turns back to Charlene, his gaze locking onto hers with an intensity that sends a quiet thrill through the air. "Are you ready?" he asks, his voice low, rich with an unspoken invitation. He pulls on a cozy, long-sleeved hoodie, his movements deliberate—like he's savoring the moment, drawing it out just a little longer.

Charlene blinks, her mind catching up to the weight in his question. "Ready? Oh, uh—yes, ready to go," she stammers, suddenly more aware of the space between them.

A slow smile tugs at Allen's lips. Without hesitation, he reaches for her hand, his fingers warm and steady around hers. Charlene barely has time to process the unexpected gesture before they step out of the studio together, the night air meeting them like the start of something new.

Chapter 16

Allen and Charlene sit in another coffee shop, where the atmosphere is lively and bustling. The aroma of freshly brewed coffee filled the air, mingling with the scent of freshly baked pastries, which Charlene sees as a very inviting treat after her exciting moments in Allen's dressing room. The atmosphere in the coffee shop is vibrant and inviting, the perfect backdrop for them to enjoy.

Charlene and Allen discuss a range of topics, from his modest beginnings in show business to his agent's remarkable talent for turning good news into "we'll circle back."

Charlene wants to bring up the subject of Allen's relationship with Gina, but she knows it is a delicate topic, and at this point, as warm and inviting as a cool breeze of a polar wind. She doesn't want to make Allen uncomfortable or make herself seem too nosy; she feels she must know. She approaches it gingerly: "Hey, Allen, I want to ask you something. You know Gina Tarvec, right?"

"Uh, huh," Allen agrees, his body slightly tensing.

"Well, you two have been seen together a lot lately. And I was wondering how you met... Are you seeing each other?"

Noticing the rather intrusive direction their conversation was heading, Allen pauses, and, almost chuckling, he asks, "You're not a reporter, are you?"

Suddenly, he had a moment of recollection. Looking more closely at her face, Allen says, "I knew I'd seen you before. You were one of the reporters hounding me the day I got back into town."

Feeling cornered, Charlene knows she must be honest with him. So, she takes a deep breath and finally reveals her secret: "Allen, I am a celebrity news reporter for CandidExposé News. And I am reporting on your relationship with Gina."

Allen's expression shifts from surprise to contemplation as he processes her words. "So, you've been watching me, then?" he asks, a hint of a smirk playing at the corners of his mouth. "I should have known you were a reporter."

Charlene bites her lip, feeling a mix of embarrassment and relief. "I know it sounds intrusive, but I didn't want to invade your privacy. I just wanted to do my job."

"Your job," he echoes, his gaze steady. "And what if I said I'm not interested in being your next headline?"

She can feel her heart racing. "I wouldn't report anything you didn't want me to," she assures him, her voice softening. "I just... I want to understand you, not just as a celebrity but as a person."

Allen's expression softens slightly, and he crosses his arms. "So, what do you want to know?"

Charlene takes another deep breath, trying to navigate this delicate moment. "What's the truth about you and Gina? Is it serious, or is it just for show?"

He hesitates for a moment, weighing his words. "Honestly? It's complicated. But, it's not what people think." Feeling betrayed, Allen stands and says, "I've got to go." He excuses himself from the table.

"Allen?" Charlene calls softly.

"Look, let me get back to you," says Allen as he pauses in his thoughts and then leaves through the door.

She calls out to Allen again, but her pleas are met only by the cold back of his retreating figure. His deliberate avoidance is palpable.

Confusion gives way to a sting of rejection. Charlene feels a hollow emptiness, a sinking sensation in the pit of her stomach, as she watches him walk away. It isn't just the act of his leaving that hurts; it is the stark contrast of shared memories, of laughter and camaraderie, against this present moment of deliberate distance.

Feeling betrayed, Charlene's heart feels heavy. The bustling cafe seems to blur around her as her focus hones in on Allen's retreating form. She clutches her coffee cup a little tighter, the warmth of the drink a stark contrast to the cold void she feels inside. The chasm between them, in that fleeting moment, feels as vast as an ocean, and she is left to grapple with the waves of disbelief and hurt that crash upon her.

That night, they both take the time to think about what is going on with him, with her, between them. They each sit in silence, lost in their own thoughts. Allen can't shake the feeling that something is off between them, and Charlene can't help but wonder if he is still invested in their relationship.

Charlene is at home, sitting at her desk. The atmosphere is calm and quiet, with a soft glow from the desk lamp illuminating the room. The air is still, and a faint scent of freshly brewed coffee lingers. The room is tidy and organized, with books neatly arranged on the shelves and a few framed photographs adorning the walls. The ticks of a clock fill the silence, creating a rhythmic backdrop to her thoughts. She stares blankly at the computer screen, knowing she must write a story, but her mind is consumed with thoughts of Allen. Had she crossed a line? Had she become too involved?

Val and Clay's warnings echo in her mind. How often have they warned her not to get too familiar with the subject? She knows she can't afford to get too close. But the pull is too strong. She can't resist the temptation to explore the depths of Allen's character. With her mind completely consumed by Allen, she embarks on a typing odyssey, organizing data and typing some more. It's as if she's been awake since the invention of the keyboard, tirelessly clacking away like a caffeinated squirrel on a mission. At last, having tired herself enough, she wraps up her project for the night; she's convinced she's pulled an all-nighter just by the sheer feeling of typing for centuries.

She picks up a book from the nearby bookshelf, walks to the bed, and slides herself under the sheets. She tries to read herself to sleep. With her mind so full of thoughts, she places her book on her face to block out any distractions. The next morning, she wakes up to find the book has somehow ended up on her head like a hat.

Charlene gets up and stands in the window, gazing out, watching the billowing clouds pass by. She pauses and then sits on the living room couch with her eyes fixed on the silent cell phone. Every passing second feels like an eternity as she waits for it to ring. The anticipation is overwhelming. She chuckles to herself, feeling silly as the realization slowly sinks in - a watched phone never rings. Yet the silence is deafening, and she can't help but feel a sense of frustration and impatience. She begins to question whether she missed the call or if something went wrong. She flips her phone around, inspecting it for damage that might prevent it from ringing, but there is none.

But as time goes on, she reluctantly accepts the truth – the call she has been waiting for may never come.

"Ugh!" Charlene groans, cupping her face in her hands before declaring, "I need to get some air."

Charlene is determined to go for a jog, continuing her revived occupation, but jogging the trails feels desolate without Allen by her side. Every stride feels heavier as if burdened by the weight of his absence, as if the path has now turned into a marshy swamp, and with each step, she sinks deeper. The once invigorating activity now feels like a lonely journey through an empty landscape. She eagerly searches through the trails, hoping to catch a glimpse of Allen. However, despite her efforts, she does not see him. Have the warnings of her coworkers about getting too close to the subject now come to bite her?

Charlene goes to the first coffee shop she and Allen had been to together, half hoping to find him there. But he isn't there either. The floral prints on the chairs appear to have lost a little of their vibrancy today. Charlene feels a mix of emotions as she turns to walk out of the coffee shop alone for the first time since she met Allen. However, there is also a tinge of sadness, as she realizes that their time together has come to an end. Feeling the slight pang of loneliness, she is beginning to wonder if this is more than a story.

Chapter 17

J ust as she turns, she hears Clay's friendly voice calling out, "There you are! Where have you been? I was looking everywhere for you yesterday. You remember the stake-out, right? Well, we're supposed to be at Allen's again tonight."

"Uh, yeah," says Charlene, snapping out of her deep thoughts.

"Come on," he says. Hopping out of the van and holding the driver-side door open for Charlene.

"Uh, yeah, just a moment," Charlene says as she gazes through the windows at the coffee shop once more.

Honk, honk! Clay is impatiently leaning on the van's horn.

Charlene's reaction to the loud sound of the van's horn is nothing short of comical. As the piercing noise echoes through the air, her eyes widen in surprise, her mouth forming a perfect "O" shape. In a split second, she jumps a foot off the ground, her hands flailing in the air for balance. The sheer shock on her face is priceless, as if she had just witnessed a magic trick gone wrong. It took her a moment to regain her composure, but once she did, she couldn't help but burst into laughter, the sound infectious and filling the air. It is a truly hilarious moment that has Clay in stitches. They get back to work in the van. Sitting in the van in front of Allen's place, Clay notices Charlene's unusual quiet.

"What's going on? Why are you so quiet? This is not like you. What did you do?" Clay asks suspiciously.

"We're not going there, Clay. We are watching Allen's place," Charlene states assertively in an attempt to steer the conversation back to a more professional tone.

Clay almost gasps, "Does this have something to do with the other night? I told you not to get involved. Getting too close doesn't end well."

"Clay!" she says, turning away and shaking her head.

"Did you kiss him?"

"Clay, this isn't a movie!"

"No, really. How far did this go?" Clay asks with one eyebrow up.

Clay can see the wheels turning in Charlene's mind as she struggles to find an explanation for the events that have unfolded. How could she justify those moments without hearing the all-too-familiar phrase, "I told you so"?

Suddenly, there is a knock on the driver's side door; it's Allen. Clay immediately puts his head back, pretending to be half asleep - a possum trick he does when they are caught.

Charlene is caught up in the whirlpool of her emotions, her thoughts racing with both elation and the lingering sense of abandonment. Allen's unexpected appearance takes her by surprise. It seems that he has decided that the silent treatment has run its course, and he's finally ready to engage in a conversation.

Charlene's heart races as she catches her first glimpse of Allen again. The mixture of emotions swirling within her is palpable. At first, a surge of relief washes over her, just knowing that he is safe and back in her presence. But that initial relief quickly gives way to a complex blend of feelings.

She feels a wave of frustration and anxiety, tinged with a hint of irritation. Questions and concerns about his disappearance without a word of explanation had gnawed at her during a long day of waiting.

However, beneath the frustration, there was an undeniable undercurrent of love and longing. Seeing him again stirred up a deep, unshakable affection that she couldn't deny. She missed his warmth, his embrace, his quirky humor, and the shared laughter they had once enjoyed.

As she sat there, her eyes locked with his, Charlene couldn't help but wear a complex expression, a mix of concern, love, and curiosity. She was eager to hear his explanation. She momentarily loses sight of the importance of maintaining her professional composure, swings the van door open, and hops out, angrily asking, "What is wrong with you? Is that what you are going to do now, take off? Disappear? I was really worried about you. How could you do that to me?

Clay sat hunched in his seat, listening intently and thinking, "Maybe this is a bigger story than I realized."

Allen responded: "I didn't intend to hurt you. But come on, you didn't tell me that you are a reporter. You being a reporter is not a big secret that you can't tell me. That's not the way this works. The way this works is that you tell me that you are a reporter. And I decide if I'm going to bolt. You get it? I decide."

After a few moments of half-hearted protests, Charlene relented, finally admitting to herself that maybe, just maybe, this time Allen is right.

Charlene and Allen stand in hushed silence. It appears that Charlene's verbal skills have temporarily run dry.

"And who's that?" asks Allen, gesturing to Clay.

"That's my cameraman, Clay. I'm a reporter, and he's my cameraman," Charlene reiterates.

Turning his attention back to Charlene, Allen says, smiling, "I knew it had to be you. I kept seeing this van, and I finally put two and two together."

"I mean, like we were here forever," says Charlene, incredulously.

"I know," says Allen, smiling.

Out of the blue, Gina saunters up to the van, oozing an air of sophistication and grace that could rival even the most glamorous supermodels, and says, "Hello. Who is this? Introduce us, Allen."

"Gina, this is Charlene, my friend, and reporter for CandidExposé News. Charlene, my friend, Gina."

"Hmm, a reporter friend," Gina thinks. "Charmed," she says elegantly.

"Same," responds Charlene.

Clay finally peeks open his eyes, and seeing them all together, quietly encourages Charlene, "They're there together, Charlene. Get the interview. Get. The. Interview. Get the interview, or I'll eat my hat. I'm not wearing a hat. Get the interview."

"I'm glad to see you," Allen says to Charlene.

"I am glad to see you, too."

"Sorry, I disappeared on you. I had to. I needed time to process what was going on. You're a reporter. I didn't know."

"What would you have done if I had told you that I am a reporter?" asks Charlene.

Gina chimes in with an unmistakably nasal giggle, "He would have sprinted like a caffeinated cheetah."

"Ok, yeah," says Allen, "I would've run. "

"Well, looks like you finally found something that you don't want to run away from," says Gina.

Allen gives Gina the look that says, "Alright, I got it! Thanks."

Charlene, realizing that maybe she had taken a misstep as she has fallen in love with this handsome, kind of hammy actor, admits, "I found you attractive. And I realize now that I was getting too personal, and that was wrong. I was not being professional."

"Well," Gina says, understanding Charlene's quandary. "You were not that professional," she says, softening the impact of the words.

Charlene and Allen hug.

"Oh, this is so romantic, Allen," says Gina, "better than some of your movies."

"And no more vanishing acts!" Charlene declares, shaking her hands with an exaggerated magician's flourish, for emphasis.

"Alright, alright," Allen chuckles and shrugs.

Recognizing that this is the ideal opportunity to obtain some answers, Charlene asks, "What's going on with you and Gina?"

Allen tells Charlene, "Of course. I have a long-time friendship with Gina, and she's been through a lot with her family. These past few months, they've been having a financial crisis. I am just helping her through it."

"Well, what about the kissing? That tells me you're a couple," says Charlene.

Allen looks over at Gina, "Gina?"

Feeling cornered, "What?" Gina asks.

Allen checks his broken watch, pats his foot impatiently, and returns his gaze to Gina.

Gina relents, throwing her shoulders up, "I like to mess with the reporters. They're so nosy. I give them something to put their noses in. It's all in good fun."

"She likes the attention," Allen says.

"You like the attention," she laughs.

Allen thinks, "Well, it does help promote my movies," as he shrugs his shoulders and shakes his head.

Charlene looks at them both and says, "You all are practical jokers, aren't you?"

Gina adds, "And for him to share his thoughts with you, dear, there must be something special between you. Because he doesn't share his thoughts with just anyone."

"Then, are you seeing anyone?" Charlene coyly asks.

Allen gives Charlene a little smirk. "I thought I was."

Charlene offers a gentle smile first to Allen, then to Gina, "Gina, I hope everything is working out for you and your family," she says.

"Yes, of course, dear."

Although Charlene is concerned for Gina, she finds that she is relieved that Allen is not seeing Gina, it looks like he's free. Allen takes Charlene's hand. "Charlene," he says, "I missed you. After I got my thoughts together, I started looking for you. But then I realized that you would be here. I figured it was probably you in the van." Allen gently sweeps a couple of wayward hair strands away from Charlene's eyes.

"I missed you, too," responded Charlene. "And, Allen, I know you didn't want to share Gina's business. And I understand, and I can respect that."

Allen and Gina both smile.

"But, Allen, you do know I am a celebrity news reporter," Charlene says, presenting her badge. "I'm going to share all your business. And hers, too, if I get hold of it."

"Yes, I know," Allen laughs.

"If," says Gina, suggesting that it might be a challenge to interview her. "Lovely to meet you, Charlene. I'll let you two be alone."

Having heard everyone's story, Clay steps out of the van, his nerves giving way to resolve. With newfound confidence, he strides over to Gina, excited to meet her. He finds her strikingly beautiful, and he is determined to introduce himself. "H-hi, I'm Clay," he says nervously. "I work with Charlene." Not wanting to let her walk alone at this hour, he offers to walk her to her limo. Flattered by his gentlemanly gesture, Gina smiles and agrees. Gina gives Allen a satisfied smile, turns, slips her arm into Clay's, and together they walk arm-in-arm to her limo, the evening air thick with the promise of something new.

Charlene could not resist picturing their lives together: Gina with her nasal chuckle, and Clay trying to feed her like a bird from his mouth. Charlene holds back a laugh, and then remembers: "Should I ask her for an interview?" she asks Allen.

Allen gently takes Charlene's chin and gazes into her eyes. "We'll work something out," he says reassuringly.

Charlene's smile deepens, a spark of anticipation flickering in her eyes. Allen, drawn to her warmth, begins to close the space between them, his breath a soft whisper against her skin as he leans in, his lips hovering just inches from hers.

Just then, they hear a wrapping on the other side of the van. It's Clay's friends coming by to chide with Clay again. Duffy makes his way over to the driver's side, excited to meet Allen Howser, a famous movie star and action hero. "Hey, it's Allen Howser. Yeah!" He throws Allen a couple of air punches, then turns to Charlene and asks, "So, what about it?"

"What about what?" responds Charlene as if she didn't know.

"Can I get your number?" Duffy asks.

Allen looks at Charlene and smiles. Charlene gives Allen a reassuring nod. And then Allen says, "No, boys. We're together."

Charlene and Allen smile at each other, hold hands for a moment, gaze into each other's eyes, and kiss.

It was such a beautiful moment, even Duffy had to smile and cheer them on.

The next day, as Val wraps up reading Charlene's article aloud, a wave of excitement sweeps through the office — everyone suddenly realizes Charlene and Allen Howser are officially a couple.

"Finally!" Val exclaims to Charlene over the excited office cheers. Everyone congratulates Charlene, giving her supportive pats on the back.

The atmosphere crackles with excitement. Everyone's on the edge of their swivel chairs, craving official confirmation of this lovey-dovey spectacle. The office is now a swirling cauldron of debates about whether Charlene and Allen's compatibility is more shocking than discovering Bigfoot working as a barista.

Speculation runs wild with colleagues unleashing their inner Sherlock Holmes, deducing everything from the couple's preferred pizza toppings to how their newfound romance might impact the office dynamics. It's like a game of 'Romantic Clue,' and the whole place is buzzing with conspiracy theories. There's so much excitement that colleagues bring pizza and balloons and turn it into a party.

Horace walks over to Charlene's cubicle.

"You did it," Horace says. "You have just topped your best article. That's a home run."

Charlene smiles.

"Finally," Horace says with a mocking grin.

"Hey!" Charlene exclaims.

"Let's celebrate," Horace says. He gives her a smile and a reassuring nod. Then he turns and leaves Charlene's cubicle.

Val looks at Charlene with a big grin. Val's big metal earrings clang as she turns her head. "You did it," Val says with a smile.

"Yeah, I did it."

"You go, Charlene!" Clay says, peering into the cubicle, followed closely by a smiling Gina. Charlene stands up, hugs Clay, and says, "Thank you, Clay."

Gina also hugs her, smiling and saying, "Congratulations, dear."

"Yeah. You even got Horace to come to your cubicle this time," Val says, emphasizing the word your. "And you know, he doesn't do that. That's not a Horace thing to do. It's like you got the royal treatment. So, it's a big deal, Charlie."

"Yeah," says Charlene in agreement, realizing that after everything, the story is actually a hit.

For a moment, Val stood silently, smiling and giving Charlene a strange glare.

"What?" Charlene asks.

"And I am closer to becoming an auntie," Val sings loudly and off-key.

"Val," Charlene laughs. "You're far ahead of me."

"We're going to CroonEoke's tonight," Val declares.

"Sounds good to me," Charlene says.

Val and Charlene rejoin the celebration, laughing and chatting, their excitement contagious. Charlene grins, knowing it's a night to remember—full of surprises and stories that are just beginning.

Chapter 18

Share Your Thoughts

Your thoughts are an important way you can help me to improve and grow the stories. Thanks. With much love, XXX

Lisa Lantree